WALT DISNEY'S
THE MISADVENTURES OF
MERLIN JONES

Based on the screenplay by
Tom and Helen August

told by Mary Carey

illustrated by
Robert L. Schaar

WHITMAN PUBLISHING COMPANY • Racine, Wis.

Contents

1   ENTER MERLIN JONES

It was opening day at Midvale College, and Officer Caedmon P. Lightfoot was perfectly miserable. Officer Lightfoot, or Ole Caddy, as he was called by the Midvale students, hated opening day. "It's not that I mind college kids," he explained to anyone in the police station who would listen. "It's just that there are so darn many of them—and they're all on wheels!"

"Take it easy, Caddy," soothed the desk sergeant.

"And if they don't have cars themselves," continued Caddy, "they've got parents with them who do. And they don't know where the girls' dorm is. And they don't know where the administration building is. And they try to turn left across the town square and jam up traffic from here to a year from next week!"

The desk sergeant turned a page in his paperback detective novel. "This, too, shall pass," he said quietly.

"Sure it will," snapped Caddy. "Opening day will pass. Then we'll have the big game, and homecoming day—that's always fun. And then the night of the junior prom. And the night of the senior prom. And the day before Christmas vacation, and the day after Christmas vacation."

"How about spring holidays?" prompted the desk sergeant.

"Nuts!" snarled Caddy. Picking up his motorcycle helmet, he slammed out of the station.

Caddy mounted his motorcycle for the half-block ride to the town square. He arrived in the square just in time to see a harassed and bewildered man in a big Buick attempt to turn left across the square. Traffic squealed to a halt.

"You can't turn there!" thundered Caddy. He revved his motorcycle and made his way expertly through a maze of stalled cars. "You can't turn there," he shouted again at the red-faced man. In the seat next to the driver, a plump woman made clicking sounds with her tongue against her teeth. The thin, long-haired girl in the back seat pulled at the driver's collar. "Daddy, I think it's the other way," she said nervously.

"Pull over to the curb." Caddy waved his arm. "Let some of these cars get by."

Perspiring profusely, the man pulled over. Caddy waved again and the traffic jam eased a bit.

Caddy leaned against the Buick. "Now, what seems to be the trouble?" he asked with pained patience.

"Officer, we are trying to find Compton Hall," said the driver.

"The girls' residence hall," put in his wife.

"At Midvale!" squeaked the youngster in the back seat. Obviously a freshman, decided Caddy.

"Oh, sure. The girls' dorm." Caddy was all brisk competence. "You go straight on through the square," he explained, "and down Morrison Road to Schenley. Take a right there to the top of the hill and. . . ."

Caddy stopped, suddenly aware that he was failing to hold his audience. The driver of the Buick was staring past Caddy; he had let his mouth drop open. In the town square a man shouted something Caddy couldn't quite catch, and a woman laughed a shrill, slightly hysterical laugh. Horns blasted.

"Green exhaust! How cool!" breathed the girl in the back seat.

Green exhaust!

Caddy felt a numb foreboding settle over him. Green

exhaust! Could it possibly be . . . ?

Caddy turned to face the square.

It was! It was Merlin Jones!

What's more, it was Merlin Jones, bright-eyed and unconcerned, carefully easing his way through the town square in a pale blue convertible. From the tail pipe of the car rose a vivid, yellow-green cloud.

"Pull over!" Caddy yelled. Then he blew his whistle and yelled again. "You—Merlin Jones! Pull over!"

Merlin pulled over.

"And cut that motor!"

Merlin cut it.

Caddy adjusted his gunbelt and stalked to the blue convertible. "Back for another year, I see," he said with grim cheer.

"You bet, Cad—er, Officer Lightfoot," said the boy in the blue convertible.

"Brainy science major like you, I thought you'd be at M.I.T. by now. As a matter of fact, I *prayed* you would." Caddy pulled out his citation pad. "I suppose you've got no idea why I stopped you?"

"Well . . . well, no, I don't," admitted Merlin Jones.

Caddy glared at Merlin, then at his car. "You're a

menace!" he accused. "A distracting menace. You might be a bigger traffic hazard on a pink elephant, but I doubt it. Green exhaust! Let me see your license."

Resignedly, Merlin dug for his wallet. "The exhaust is just the result of an exper . . ." he began to explain.

"I know. Don't tell me. An experiment!"

"That's right." Merlin handed over his driver's license. "With certain additives in the fuel, and the carburetor set for—"

"Please!" Caddy winced. "Please don't tell me. Tell it to the judge, if you want to. You'll be seeing him tomorrow morning at ten o'clock. Sign the ticket."

Merlin signed and Caddy tore off the summons. "Before I see you again," he warned, "you'd better make that car stop that—that—whatever it's doing." And Caddy walked away.

"How perfectly idiotic!"

Merlin's head swiveled toward the sidewalk.

"Unfair, too!" said a dark-haired girl standing there. Her eyes flashed. "I'll bet there's not a thing in the Constitution about exhaust having to be black!"

"No, I suppose not," agreed Merlin.

"I think green exhaust is attractive," added the girl.

"Thanks. Thanks a lot." Merlin noticed all at once that she was quite small, and very pretty—and she was carrying a bulky suit box. He scrambled out of the car.

"Can I help you with that?" He snatched the box. "Can I give you a lift anywhere?"

"That would be nice." While Merlin held the door, she got into the car and smoothed down her red skirt. "My name is Jennifer," she said. "Jennifer Hartley."

Merlin tossed the box into the back of the car and slid behind the wheel. "I'm Merlin Jones."

"I know. Everybody for three blocks around knows —after the way that policeman yelled at you."

Merlin chuckled. "Caddy doesn't have much scientific curiosity."

"From what I hear," said Jennifer, "neither does Judge Holmsby."

"Yeah." Merlin put the car into gear. "He was pretty hard-nosed last year when. . . ."

"When what?"

"Oh, nothing. It was just a litle misunderstanding about a siren, but he suspended my license." Anxious to change the subject, Merlin glanced sideways at the girl. "You're new at Midvale," he ventured.

She nodded. "I had my freshman year at State. Then Daddy's company transferred him here, so I'll be at Midvale for my sophomore year, at least. We live out on Oakdale Drive."

Merlin turned his car west out of the square. "You'll like Midvale," he predicted.

"I hope so. It's a little scary, entering in the sophomore year. And living off the campus. . . ."

"Nothing to worry about." Merlin's voice was cheerful. "Lots of us live off campus. I stay at Mrs. Schmidt's, over on Keystone. It's good for the budget. Besides, she's nice, and she's an old friend of my uncle."

"Your uncle?"

"Nostradamus P. Jones, Midvale, class of '23. I looked him up in the old '23 yearbook in the library after I got here. Do you know, they used to call him Perpetual-Motion Jones!"

"Why?"

"Because he wanted to invent a perpetual-motion machine."

"Did he?"

Merlin chuckled. "Hardly. He gave up the battle and went into the insurance business. But he still likes to tinker. We have a lab at home—a little one. We were working out this—this thing, all summer."

"You mean the green exhaust?"

"Yes. But that wasn't exactly the idea. The real trick is to have no exhaust at all. We haven't got all the bugs out of it yet, as you can tell."

"Oh, I don't know. It's an improvement on the regular stuff."

"Depends on your viewpoint. Say, how far out on Oakdale do you live?"

"Near the reservoir," said Jennifer. "I guess you must spend a lot of time with your uncle."

"I guess so," Merlin confirmed. "He brought me up after my parents died."

"Oh, I'm sorry," said Jennifer softly.

"Don't be." Merlin's grin was a bit crooked. "I was so young when it happened that I don't even remember a mother and father. You can't miss what you never had—or can you?"

"I don't know," said Jennifer.

"This the block?" Merlin was quickly businesslike.

"Yes. The brown house, halfway down."

The convertible glided smoothly up to the curb.

"Thanks for driving me home," said Jennifer warmly. "Won't you come in for a minute?"

Merlin tugged her package from the back seat and went around the car to open the door. "I don't think I'd better. I want to go check in with Mrs. Schmidt before she rents my room to some downy-cheeked freshman. Nice to meet you, Jennifer. Everyone does call you Jennifer, I suppose?"

She laughed. "No, everyone calls me Jen. Except my mother. She calls me Jennie sometimes."

"Okay, Jen. I'll see you around."

"Yes, you will," Jen murmured to herself as she went up the front steps.

Jennifer found her mother in the living room, peering after Merlin's car from behind the slats of the venetian blind. "Who drove you home, dear?" Mrs. Hartley asked pleasantly. She was not at all upset at being caught peeking.

"Merlin Jones. He goes to Midvale."

"Oh? He looks like a nice boy."

"I think he is."

"I've always liked dark-haired men." Mrs. Hartley was hopelessly romantic.

Jennifer could see that her mother was extremely curious. "His eyes are blue," she supplied.

"That's good. But there was something odd about his car, Jennie. Do you really think you should have ridden in it?"

"I'm sure it's perfectly safe, Mother. And he's a very good driver."

"But the exhaust. Surely you must have noticed. The exhaust is green!"

"Not really, Mother. I think it's more chartreuse, don't you? Is my good black suit home from the cleaners?"

"Your black suit? What does that have to do. . . ."

"I want to go downtown tomorrow morning."

"Oh. Well, it's in the back closet. The hem needs a stitch or two. You must have caught your heel. . . ."

"I'll fix it."

Jen was starting up the stairs when her father swung into the drive. "Mollie!" he bellowed from the front yard. "Jennifer! I just saw the darndest thing!"

Jen and her mother hurried to the door.

"I passed a blue convertible on the road." Mr. Hartley waved his briefcase in the general direction of town.

"And it was spouting green exhaust!"

Mrs. Hartley nodded. "I know, Harold. That was Jennifer's friend."

"Jennifer's friend?"

"Merlin Jones."

Mr. Hartley spluttered. "Mollie! Make sense. No one is named Merlin Jones."

"Merlin is," said Jen calmly. "He's Nostradamus P. Jones's nephew."

Mr. Hartley's face began to take on a peculiar tinge of red. "And just who is Nostradamus P. Jones?" he demanded.

"Midvale, class of '23," explained Jennifer. "They called him Perpetual-Motion Jones." She went back into the house and started up the stairs again. Her father hurried after her.

"Don't tell me he invented perpetual motion," he challenged.

"No," said Jen sadly. "He went into the insurance business." And she disappeared into the back bedroom.

2

At exactly ten the next morning, Jennifer, carefully dressed in her best black suit, slipped into one of the rear seats in Judge Holmsby's courtroom. Court was already in session, and the Honorable Curtice C. Holmsby, black-gowned and unsmiling, was listening with weary dignity as a wiry little man in faded overalls attempted to explain how he happened to have three of his neighbor's prize Plymouth Rock hens locked in his garage.

There were few spectators in the courtroom, and Jen quickly located Merlin in the second row. He seemed completely absorbed in the testimony of the accused chicken thief.

"So you see, yer Honor," the man was saying, "I just locked them hens up so they wouldn't wander out in the road and get run over, er nothin'."

With the point of a pencil, Judge Holmsby tapped a report that lay in front of him. "Then, Mr. Perkins,

you really intended to return the hens to their owner?"
The judge's voice dripped with disbelief.

"Why, sure. I was goin' to, yer Honor. Jest as soon as
I got time."

"And for three whole days you were so busy you
hadn't a moment to attend to this?"

The unfortunate Perkins coughed miserably. "I . . .
er . . . well, what with one thing and 'nother, time
slipped by. You know how it is."

"Indeed I know how it is." The judge consulted his
papers again. "And you contend that you did not re-
move a board from the fence separating your property
from your neighbor's with the express intention of lur-
ing the chickens into your yard?"

"Oh, I took the board out, all right," said Perkins.
"It was rotten. I was gonna put in a new one jest as
soon as. . . ."

Judge Holmsby frowned fiercely. Perkins' voice
wavered and died.

"As soon as you had time," the judge finished the
sentence.

"That's right, yer Honor."

"I see." The judge sighed. "Mr. Perkins, you have

not been in my court before today?"

"No, yer Honor."

"Very well. Since that is the case, and since the hens have been returned to their rightful owner, I am prepared to dismiss the charges this time."

Perkins brightened up.

"Next time you will not fare so well," warned the judge.

"There won't be no next time," promised Perkins.

"I sincerely hope not. You may go, Mr. Perkins."

The man turned and ambled toward the door. The judge rapped sharply with his pencil. "Next case."

"Merlin Jones!" shouted the court clerk.

Merlin rose and took his place before the bench.

Judge Holmsby barely glanced at Merlin. Instead, he shuffled through his papers. "Mr. Jones," he began, "you are charged with creating a traffic hazard in the town square. Would you care to explain this to the court?"

"It wasn't really a hazard, your Honor," said Merlin. "Just something a little different."

"Oh?" The judge's eyebrows shot toward his hairline. "Perhaps Officer Lightfoot can give us a little more information about this. Will the clerk call the officer, please?"

"Officer Caedmon P. Lightfoot!" intoned the clerk.

Caddy lurched from his seat in the spectators' section of the courtroom and came forward to stand beside Merlin.

"Now, Officer Lightfoot, please tell us what was going on in the town square yesterday afternoon when you gave Mr. Jones this citation," instructed the judge.

"Certainly, your Honor." Caddy cleared his throat importantly. "Yesterday was opening day at Midvale, and traffic in the square was heavy, like always on opening day."

Judge Holmsby nodded.

"But it was moving okay until this—this Merlin Jones came along."

"And Mr. Jones stopped traffic?" questioned the judge.

"He nearly caused a riot! Him and his green exhaust!"

The judge suddenly sat up straighter. "Green exhaust?"

"Yes, your Honor. He was driving a blue convertible

with green exhaust coming out of it."

The judge shuddered. "Is this true, Mr. Jones?"

"Yes, sir," admitted Merlin. "I've been experiment-ing with certain hydrocarbons. . . ."

"Please, Mr. Jones," the judge cut in, "I do not wish to learn how you arrived at green exhaust. It is enough just knowing. . . . It is enough to know. . . ." The judge stopped and a puzzled look crossed his face. "Mr. Jones, have you been in this courtroom before?" he asked.

Merlin nodded.

"I cited him last spring," said Caddy, "for unauthor-ized use of a siren on a motor vehicle."

"Ah, yes. I remember now."

"That wasn't really a siren, sir," Merlin explained quickly. "A siren produces its tone by interrupting a current of air with rotating perforated disks. I found a way of getting the same tone by an entirely new principle, so technically it really couldn't be called a siren."

"Did it sound like a siren?" said the judge.

"Yes, sir," Merlin said brightly.

"Then in the eyes—and ears—of the law, it was a

siren. Now to come back to the affair of yesterday afternoon, you must have realized that green clouds rising from your car would distract motorists and pedestrians alike, creating a traffic hazard and a public nuisance."

In the back of the courtroom, Jennifer decided that Merlin needed some help. She slid quickly from her seat and hurried toward the bench, her high heels making outraged little clicks on the terrazzo floor. "Your Honor, if you please," she said softly.

"Yes, young lady. Have you something to add to this discussion?"

"Your Honor." Jen could feel her face getting hot. "I'm here as a . . . an *amicus curiae*."

"A friend of the court?" The judge groaned. "Good heavens! What next?"

"I was in the town square yesterday when Merlin got that ticket," Jennifer persisted.

"Well?"

"And Merlin wasn't really being a traffic hazard at all. I mean, some people did blow their horns at him and laugh, but some people laugh at anything, your Honor. And the exhaust wasn't really green—it was more chartreuse, and really kind of pretty, even if it

didn't go with the blue car very well. Besides, it doesn't say anywhere in the vehicle code that exhaust has to be gray, does it?"

Judge Holmsby felt that he was about to have a headache—a very severe headache. "What is your name, young woman?" he demanded.

Having steeled herself and made her protest, Jen felt her courage leave her. "Jennifer Hartley, sir," she said in a very small voice.

"You are, I assume, a student at the college?"

"Yes, sir."

"Taking pre-law?"

"No, sir. English lit."

"I should have known. Whether you know it or not, Miss Hartley, you are *not* here as a friend of the court. You are obviously here as a friend of Merlin Jones. Now I suggest that you sit down and keep quiet."

Jennifer sat down.

The judge turned to Merlin. "Now, Mr. Jones, let us finish with this deplorable business as quickly as possible. As Miss Hartley has pointed out, there is nothing in the vehicle code to the effect that exhaust must be gray. However, there is a great deal in the code to the effect that an automobile must be operated in a safe and sensible manner. I am willing to dismiss the charge against you, since it is faintly possible—just *faintly* possible—that you really did not know how the good citizens of Midvale would react at the sight of your, er, your green exhaust."

"Thank you, your Honor."

"All right, Mr. Jones. You may go. And I do hope we will not meet again."

"I hope not, sir."

Merlin left the courtroom, closely followed by Jennifer. In the corridor he stopped to grin at her. "Thanks a lot, Jen," he said simply.

Jennifer tried to grin back, and found that she couldn't quite do it. "I'm afraid I wasn't much help." She shook her head ruefully. "My, he's a stiff one. I felt like a complete idiot!"

"You were just great! Come on, I'll buy you a cup of coffee."

"I could use one."

In the parking lot Jen glanced worriedly at the tail pipe of Merlin's car.

"It's okay," Merlin laughed, holding the door open

for her. "I drained the tank last night and filled it with regular. No more Technicolor exhaust."

"That's good." Jen got in. "I sort of liked it, but it's not worth a visit with Judge Holmsby. Where are we going?"

"The Campus Cafe. Where else?" Merlin headed the car away from the courthouse and through the town square toward the row of small shops that clustered near the main gates of the college.

"I start work here as fifth assistant waiter and part-time busboy tomorrow," said Merlin as he nosed the car into a parking place next to the cafe. "Today I'm just another customer. Let's go."

Inside, the cafe was cool and quiet. Pine-paneled walls gleamed dimly. Rows of tables were primly set with paper place mats, steel silverware, and bone-dry water glasses. Except for a thin, hawk-faced man brooding over a cup of coffee at a table in a far corner, the place was empty.

The thin man spotted Merlin and Jen and raised a bony hand in greeting. "Jones! Welcome!"

"Hi, Professor!" Merlin shepherded Jennifer forward. "Jen, meet Professor Shattuck. He's head of the psychology department. Professor, this is Jennifer Hartley."

The professor unfolded himself from his chair, bowed briefly to Jen, held a chair for her, then sat down again.

"This place is a morgue," he announced.

Merlin agreed. "Where is everybody?"

"Unpacking, I guess. Or switching courses. Or maybe writing home for money already. Who knows? You are new here, Miss Hartley?"

"Yes," said Jen. "I'm from State. I'll be a sophomore this year."

The professor nodded. "Fine. Then you'll be taking my Psychology II course."

"Oh, but I hadn't. . . ."

"Now, Miss Hartley, you must take Psych II. It's great fun! And this year I have a real treat for you. For experiments in psychology, the college has finally acquired a chimpanzee!"

"No kidding, Professor!" To Jennifer's amazement, Merlin seemed almost as pleased about this as the professor.

"You see, Jen," Merlin hastened to explain, "up till now Professor Shattuck has had only rats and hamsters to work with in his psychology experiments. But a chimpanzee is much better. The chimpanzee is the highest of manlike apes."

"How nice!" said Jen.

"It is nice. Why, I'll bet that in a lot of situations a chimp would react the way you do."

"Thanks loads!"

The professor laughed. "Don't take it personally, Miss Hartley. Merlin just means that chimps are uncannily like people. Stanley certainly is."

"You've named him Stanley?"

The professor looked slightly embarrassed. "He greatly resembles a distant cousin of mine, Stanley Pierpont," he explained. "I couldn't resist the temptation, so Stanley it is."

A plump, bright-faced waitress peered around the kitchen door, then hurried forward and, without waiting for Merlin to order, clattered two coffee cups down on the table, filled them from a steaming pot, refilled the professor's cup, and vanished again.

"Effie's efficient, I'll say that," remarked Merlin.

"Suppose I'd wanted a Coke?" said Jen.

"You'd be out of luck," the professor chuckled.

The front door of the cafe banged open. Jen looked around to see a huge hulk of a young man in a letterman's sweater slam the door shut behind him and lumber across the room toward the professor's table.

"I got that monkey locked up," the newcomer announced gruffly. He pulled out a chair and sat down.

"Chimpanzee," corrected Merlin.

"And who asked you, egghead?"

"Jennifer, this delightful soul is Norman," said Merlin. "He takes care of the animals in the psych lab. He is also Midvale's own full-time, practicing campus hero, strong man, and star halfback!"

Bewildered at the sudden hostility in Merlin's voice, Jen murmured a lame how-do-you-do.

Norman, really noticing Jennifer for the first time, allowed a slow grimace to distort his flat features. "Well, wahoo!" he cried, and Jen realized that the grimace was what Norman used for a smile.

Norman's cauliflower ears reddened with pleasure as he leaned across the table. "When did you arrive?" he gurgled happily, grabbing for Jen's hand. But she was too quick for him.

The waitress scurried in from the kitchen, coffeepot

in hand, but at the sight of Norman she turned and dived back through the swinging door.

"Now what's with her?" Norman demanded.

"Maybe she's remembering the day you had so much fun sticking people with a hatpin," suggested Merlin.

"That was just a joke!"

"Some joke."

Norman jumped to his feet. "Now, listen, Jones!" he roared.

"Norman!" The professor's voice caught Norman and held him motionless.

"I wish you'd go back and check the lock on the chimp's cage," Shattuck said quietly. "It didn't look too secure to me this morning."

Muttering, Norman slammed out.

"He's grumpy today," Shattuck explained.

"He's grumpy everyday," said Merlin.

"Especially today," the professor insisted. "An oddball thing happened in the lab this morning with Norman and the chimp. I was doing a little testing with Stanley, using Norman for a control. It was one of those basic things—you know, seeing how fast the chimp could put a square peg in a square hole and a round peg in a round hole. And it was the strangest thing—a real fluke. Never happen again in a million years."

"Don't tell me," said Merlin. "Let me guess. The chimp did it better than Norman."

The professor nodded. "No explanation for a thing like that. Just a freak. I'm tearing up my notes on the whole episode. No one would believe it, anyway."

Merlin and Jen considered this in silence for a brief moment. Then Jennifer nodded firmly. "You know what?" she said.

"What?" asked Merlin.

"I believe it."

Merlin Jones entered the Hartleys' kitchen and sniffed the mingled aromas of sizzling bacon, frying eggs, toast, fresh coffee, and something else. "You've got a short in your electric percolator," he said.

"Do I? Oh, dear!" Mrs. Hartley pulled the plug from the wall socket. "I thought I smelled something funny," she admitted. "Well, at least the coffee's done for this morning."

"Want me to fix the percolator?" Merlin offered.

"Oh, could you, Merlin?"

"I can try. I'll take a look at it this afternoon."

Jennifer breezed in wearing a special morning brightness and a haze-green sweater and skirt. "Hi, Merlin!" she said. "Morning, Mother. Hey, something's burning."

"Merlin says there's a short in the coffeepot." Mrs. Hartley carried the offending percolator to the table and poured for Merlin and Jennifer.

Mr. Hartley loomed through the doorway. He was in his shirt sleeves and his cuffs flapped loose. "Mollie, will you fasten these blasted cuff links?" he demanded. "And what's on fire around here?"

"Merlin says there's a short in the coffeepot."

"Oh, he does, does he?" Mr. Hartley glared at Merlin. "Good morning, Merlin." It was not really a greeting; it was more of a challenge. Though more than two weeks had passed since the episode of the green exhaust, and though neither Merlin nor his car had exploded into any new form of bizarre behavior, Mr. Hartley continued to regard his daughter's friend with suspicion.

"Merlin's going to fix the coffeepot," announced Mrs. Hartley.

"Why?"

"Because it's broken, dear." Mrs. Hartley was calmly reasonable. "Now sit down and have your nice breakfast."

Mr. Hartley sat, and Merlin stumbled to his feet.

"Better finish your coffee," advised Mr. Hartley. "It may be the last cup you get around here for awhile."

"We really have to be going," Merlin explained. "We

have to stop and see Stanley before class."

Jennifer got up. "I'll be ready in a minute," she promised. "I'll just get my books." She vanished through the dining-room door.

"Who's Stanley?" asked Mr. Hartley.

"He's a chimpanzee," said Merlin. At Mr. Hartley's startled look, he hastened to explain, "He belongs to the college psychology department."

"I see." Mr. Hartley felt there was something vaguely subversive about visiting chimpanzees, but he couldn't quite put his finger on what it was. He shook the defective percolator at Merlin. "You're sure you can fix this?" he asked.

"I think so, sir. It shouldn't be hard."

"Of course Merlin can fix it." Mrs. Hartley beamed at her husband. "Didn't Merlin fix the television set when you couldn't turn it off?" she reminded him.

Mr. Hartley's ears began to show faint red danger signals and Merlin quickly retreated to his car.

"I don't think your father likes me," Merlin confided to Jen as they drove toward the college.

Jen smiled. "He doesn't dislike you, really," she said. "I think you make him nervous, though. What's with the early morning visit to Stanley?"

"Nothing special—except that he's been kind of off his feed lately. Professor Shattuck thinks he needs time to get used to his new surroundings. I thought I'd bring him a present to cheer him up." Merlin held up a banana.

"That's nice. You go and see Stanley and I'll meet you in class."

Merlin shot a surprised look at Jen.

"I don't want to run into Norman if I can help it," she explained.

"Has that guy been bothering you?" Merlin asked.

"Not exactly. But he does kind of follow me around."

Merlin chuckled and eased expertly into the last parking place left at the curb outside the science building. "Save me a seat, will you?" he asked Jen. "I'll be right along."

"You bet," Jen promised.

In the basement of the science building, the psych lab was deserted except for half a dozen sleek white rats, a few hamsters, and Stanley the chimpanzee, who crouched in a far corner of his cage.

"Hi, Stanley," said Merlin softly. He held out the

banana. Ignoring it, Stanley turned his back on Merlin.

"Aw, come on. Don't be like that." Merlin edged the banana through the bars of the cage. Stanley peeked over his shoulder.

"I'm your friend," Merlin assured the chimp.

Stanley's shiny, shoe-button eyes searched Merlin's face.

"That's right," encouraged Merlin. "Come on. Take the nice banana."

Stanley edged forward.

"That's a good fella," Merlin cheered him on.

Still watching Merlin's face, Stanley stretched out a long hairy arm. Merlin gently placed the banana in the chimp's hand. Stanley immediately transferred his attention from Merlin to the banana. He examined the fruit carefully, shook it, rubbed it against his cheek, sniffed it, then neatly peeled back the skin and began to eat.

"Jones!" Norman's voice boomed from the top of the stairs.

Merlin jumped. Stanley squealed with fright, threw the banana through the bars, and fled to the back of his cage.

"That monkey's had his breakfast!" Norman thundered down the stairs.

Merlin sighed. "He's a chimpanzee, not a monkey," he said, as if explaining something to a backward child.

"He's a nutty monkey," insisted Norman. "And I don't want you spoiling him—feeding him when my back's turned."

"Why not?" demanded Merlin.

"I have my reasons." Norman strode toward Stanley's cage. "You've got to be firm with them animals, or they. . . ."

Merlin was never to learn what animals would do if not treated firmly, for at that moment Norman's heel came down heavily on the remains of Stanley's banana. Norman seemed to fly upward and float for an instant before crashing down flat on his back.

Stanley gave vent to a high, apish giggle.

"That's why I don't want you feeding him," roared Norman. He lunged to his feet. "If I ever catch you giving him bananas again, Jones, I'll see that you're not allowed to use this lab! Now get out of here!"

Norman stormed off into the storeroom which adjoined the lab.

"Never mind, Stanley," Merlin told the woebegone-looking chimpanzee. "Even if I can't bring you bananas, I'll find something else you like."

Minutes later, Merlin slipped into the chair next to Jennifer's in Professor Shattuck's crowded lecture room. "I think I know what's the matter with Stanley," he whispered.

"What?" asked Jen.

"Norman," Merlin told her. "Norman doesn't like Stanley one little bit. Stanley's a sensitive animal. He's bound to react to a thing like that. When I went in there this morning he was just sitting in that cage shivering."

"Well, what are you going to do about it?"

"I don't know yet," confessed Merlin. "But I'll think of. . . ."

"Mr. Jones, are you quite through?" Professor Shattuck's voice cut across Merlin's urgent whisper.

Merlin snapped to attention.

"If you and Miss Hartley have finished your tête-à-tête, I'd like to begin my lecture," said the professor.

"I'm sorry, Professor." Merlin opened his notebook.

"Today," said Professor Shattuck, "we are going to

take up the subject of hypnosis."

A pleased stir ran through the lecture room. The professor waited until he had silence, then he began.

"Hypnosis is very old," Shattuck told his students. "Since the dawn of history there have been tales of men and women who had hypnotic powers. In ancient times, of course, these people were feared and shunned. It was said that they had the evil eye, and that there were various charms and amulets to protect one against this power. Eating garlic was supposed to ward off the evil eye. I imagine it did; at least it would tend to keep the hypnotist at a respectful distance."

Professor Shattuck was warming up, and his students rewarded him with amused titters.

"Today, science has begun to give the subject of hypnotism serious attention. Though there are many questions still to be answered, we have learned a great deal. Skilled physicians have used hypnotism as anesthesia in many cases. With hypnotism, psychiatrists have altered personality and plumbed the depths of the subconscious. It is claimed that through hypnotism a being may be helped to realize his full potential."

The professor paused and his eyes swept the room. "I

think the best introduction to the subject would be a small demonstration of just how it works," he announced. "Merlin Jones, will you come up here, please?"

Jennifer smiled encouragement as Merlin started out of his seat and went to the front of the room.

"Sit down, please." The professor pushed forward a wooden armchair. "Make yourself comfortable."

Merlin sat down.

"Are you quite comfortable?"

Merlin nodded. "Yes, sir."

"First, I want to assure you that this experience will be absolutely harmless to you," said the professor.

Merlin smiled, a little uncertainly.

"In fact, it will be rather pleasant," said Shattuck. He held up his right hand, on which a wide gold ring gleamed. "Do you see my ring?" he asked.

"Yes."

"I want you to concentrate on my ring. Keep your gaze fixed on it. Concentrate on my ring and my voice. Your entire body will begin to feel pleasantly heavy...."

Merlin, too relaxed to be surprised, soon realized that his body did indeed feel pleasantly heavy.

"You will fall into a deep sleep," said the professor.

"It will be a deep, pleasant sleep. Your eyes are very heavy now—very, very heavy, and it's difficult to keep them open."

Merlin's lids drooped.

"When I count three, you will close your eyes and immediately fall into a deep, pleasant, hypnotic sleep," said the professor, very softly.

"One!" he counted. "Two! Three!"

Merlin's eyes closed.

"Now clasp your hands together," commanded the professor.

Merlin did so.

"Your hands are locked together," said Shattuck. "No matter how hard you try, you can't separate them. Try to separate them, Merlin."

Merlin writhed and strained in his chair, but his hands remained stubbornly clasped.

"When I touch your arm, you will be able to separate your hands," the professor told him. He put his hand gently on Merlin's arm. Immediately Merlin's struggles ceased. His hands fell to his sides.

"Open your eyes."

Merlin obeyed.

"You will hear nothing but my voice," said Shattuck. "And you will hear me only when I speak directly to you. Is that clear?"

"Yes, sir."

"Good." From a desk drawer Professor Shattuck took a pistol. A nervous murmur ran through the room. "Don't worry," Shattuck told his students. "It's loaded with blanks." And, holding the gun near Merlin's ear, the professor fired.

The shot rattled the windows and brought squeals of shock from several of the girls. Merlin sat on, still as a statue.

"That seems to have awakened most of you," Shattuck told his class, "but, as you can see, he didn't hear it at all."

The professor dived back into his desk and came up with a potato. "This is scrubbed clean, ready to be cooked," he said, "but in this experiment we're going to use it raw."

He turned to Merlin. "Do you like apples?" he asked.

"Yes, sir. Very much."

"Good. I'm going to give you this apple. I want you to eat it and see if you can guess what variety it is." With a sidelong smile at the class, Professor Shattuck handed the raw potato to Merlin.

"Is it a Jonathan?" he asked Merlin. "A McIntosh? A Winesap? What kind of apple is it?"

Merlin took an enthusiastic bite out of the potato and began to chew, considering the problem carefully. "It's delicious!" he said at last.

"You think it's a Delicious apple? Now what makes you think that?"

"No, sir. Not a Delicious apple. I meant that the apple is delicious. It's the best apple I've ever tasted." Merlin took another big bite. "But I can't figure out what kind it is," he said at last.

Merlin continued to devour the potato, and the professor turned to the class. "We will try another experiment," he announced. "Miss Everhart, will you come up here?"

A pretty blond girl came from the third row and stood beside Shattuck's desk. From a pitcher which was on the desk, the professor poured water into one of several glasses. "Please taste this," said Shattuck, handing her the glass.

The girl took a sip. "It's water," she said.

"Right," said the professor. "Plain old H-two-O."

Filling another glass with water from the pitcher, he handed it to Merlin. "I've just given you a glass of whiskey," he told Merlin. "It's very strong whiskey. I want you to drink it."

Merlin hesitated, then raised the glass to his lips. At the last moment he wrinkled his nose in distaste and handed the glass back to Shattuck. "I'm sorry, sir," he said. "I don't drink."

Shattuck smiled and replaced the glass on the desk. "He resists a command that is contrary to his own basic code," he explained to the class. "Mr. Jones is not a drinker, so he rejects the hypnotic command to drink this 'whiskey.' Some authorities believe that by persistent effort an individual's moral code can be broken down. Others say that hypnosis cannot make a person do what he believes is wrong."

The professor glanced at his wristwatch. "We have time for one more experiment," he announced.

He leaned on the back of Merlin's chair. "Merlin," he began, in a most persuasive voice. "You are an extremely talented young man."

"I am?" Merlin brightened up.

"Indeed you are. Why, right now you could be the most famous rock 'n' roll singer in the country. And, Merlin, I'll tell you a little secret." The professor's voice dropped to a conspiratorial whisper. "There's a talent scout from one of the big recording companies right in the back of this lecture hall."

Merlin's eyes anxiously scanned the back of the lecture room.

"I want you to show him what you can do," urged the professor. From a cupboard in the corner he took a guitar, which he thrust at Merlin. "Here's your guitar. Now get up, Merlin, and let the talent scout see you perform."

The girl on Jennifer's left giggled as Merlin clutched the guitar and assumed a slack-kneed, slouching stance in front of the room. Jen shot her a hard stare and she quickly subsided.

Merlin twanged at the guitar strings.

"I'm a poor boy wantin' some pity," he moaned.

Roars of laughter went up from the class. Jennifer felt like a woman who suddenly discovers that her husband is the type who wears lampshades at parties.

Merlin plucked at the guitar again.

"I need your lovin' a lot,"

he lamented.

"So take me away, away with you,

Or my whole world's gone to pot."

He jerked into convulsive motion, twitching from head to toe and pounding at the guitar.

"Away, away, far, far away,

'Cause I need your lovin' a lot."

The laughter in the room went up two octaves. Unhearing, Merlin howled on and on and on, through seven tortured verses of the song. At last, sweating and gasping, he gave forth with one final, triumphant, "Far, far away," and collapsed, exhausted, against the desk.

It was a glorious finish. Professor Shattuck applauded, and so did the class.

"Very good, Merlin," laughed the professor. "I think we've demonstrated that hypnosis can help an individual develop his full potential. Maybe it can even bring out a talent that isn't there at all."

Merlin grinned foolishly.

"In just a few seconds the bell will ring, ending this class," said the professor. "Merlin, I want you to go and take your seat. When the bell rings, you will come out of the hypnotic trance. You will feel relaxed and refreshed. Do you understand?"

"Yes, sir. I understand."

"Return to your seat now," ordered Shattuck.

Merlin put the guitar on the desk and walked back to his place. As he took his chair Jennifer frowned darkly at him.

The bell rang.

"Nice going, Jones," said a jeering voice in Merlin's ear. Merlin turned to see Harvey Potts headed for the door.

"Oh, Merlin, you were a scream!" cooed Louise Everhart. She departed, trailing her giggles behind her.

"Huh?" said Merlin.

The lecture hall emptied fast. In a few moments only Merlin and Jen remained.

"Merlin Jones! I have never seen such an exhibition!" Jen exploded.

"What?"

"You looked like a perfect—a perfect idiot!"

"But, Jen, what did I do?"

"Do? You mean you don't remember?"

"No," said Merlin. "I don't remember. The last thing I recall was looking at the professor's ring. He was telling me to relax."

"Well, you relaxed all right—all over the place. You were so relaxed you did the silliest rock 'n' roll number I ever saw!"

"You're kidding."

"I'm not kidding. It was awful. Everyone just howled!"

"Aw, Jennie, don't be that way. You know I wouldn't usually do a thing like that."

"I should hope not!"

"Why, I don't even like rock 'n' . . . ." Merlin's voice trailed off.

"What is it?" said Jen.

"I was thinking," Merlin replied. "I sing like a sick bullfrog and I hate rock 'n' roll. But, using hypnosis, Professor Shattuck made me do a rock 'n' roll number in front of the whole class."

"You played a guitar, too," Jen said vengefully.

"Good night!" exclaimed Merlin. "And I can't play a guitar. But that's just the point."

"What point?"

"Hypnotism can change a being's whole personality. It can help people to rise above the circumstances of their lives—to realize their full potential! The professor said so, and he's proved it."

Jennifer recalled Merlin gyrating madly in front of the class. She shuddered. "Merlin! Don't you *dare* realize your full potential!" she warned.

"I'm not talking about me," Merlin said. "I'm talking about Stanley. I think I've got an answer to his problem. Come on, Jen. I've got some research to do!"

4 RIOT IN THE LABORATORY

Mrs. Schmidt, who was truly fond of Merlin, occasionally found herself wishing that she had rented her spare room to a business major. Merlin's tendency to take things apart to see what made them go was unnerving. True, Merlin had cured her washing machine of a chronic case of hiccups. And he had restored life to the long-silent grandfather clock on the stairs. For these favors Mrs. Schmidt was grateful. But it was also true that he had cleverly combined her electric waffle iron with parts of an old clock-radio he had found somewhere. Merlin's motivation was sound. The waffle iron would warm up automatically each morning and be ready for instant use when Mrs. Schmidt came downstairs. But a waffle iron that blared forth "The Star-Spangled Banner" each day at seven A.M. was a bit more than Mrs. Schmidt could stand. She had removed the thing to the garage and gone back to fixing pancakes on the stove.

So it was with understandable misgivings that Mrs. Schmidt saw Merlin come in that night loaded to the chin with books. Mrs. Schmidt knew Merlin only too well. A pile of books that high meant that he had a new project under way.

Mrs. Schmidt embarked upon a small fishing expedition. "My, Merlin, you have a lot of books there!" she began with enormous innocence.

"Got a lot to learn," was Merlin's only answer.

Mrs. Schmidt trailed him up the stairs. "You're just like your uncle," she said, harping on a very old refrain. "He was always trying to find out about things or change them around to something that they weren't."

"I know." Merlin went into his room and dumped the books on his desk. "He was good at it, too."

Mrs. Schmidt hovered in the doorway. "Sometimes," she admitted. "But sometimes he got into trouble. One night there was the most terrible explosion in the college chemistry lab. . . ."

Merlin, who had heard all about the explosion in the chemistry lab, understood immediately what Mrs. Schmidt was fishing for.

"I'm not working on chemistry now," he explained.

"I'm just trying to find out more about hypnosis."

She thought this over. She had seen a hypnotist once, plying his trade on the stage of the Bijou Theater down at Century City. It had seemed a silly but fairly quiet affair, and it hadn't involved mixing any chemicals or tampering with any wires. Of course, it was ridiculous to make people get up and act like chickens, but it hadn't really hurt anyone.

"Well, all right, Merlin," she said at last. "Don't stay up too late."

"I won't."

"And put Mittens out before you go to bed."

Merlin glanced at the orange and white cat curled up in the only comfortable chair in the room. "I will," he said.

"Good night, Merlin."

"Good night, Mrs. Schmidt."

She closed the door and Merlin settled down with his books. A moment later she was back.

"Merlin."

"Yes?"

"There's half an icebox cake down in the refrigerator if you're hungry."

"Thank you, Mrs. Schmidt."

She disappeared again, this time for good. Merlin smiled and opened the top book of the pile on the desk. It was a heavy tome entitled *Fundamentals of Hypnotic Techniques.*

The first chapter, Merlin found, was pretty much a thumbnail history of hypnosis. Much was said of the Dark Ages, when hypnotists were accused of witchcraft. The garlic cure for the evil eye was mentioned. Merlin flipped the pages quickly and, with the second chapter, began to get down to brass tacks.

"To induce hypnosis, present your subject with circumstances that are conducive to sleep and relaxation," read Merlin.

Mittens, the cat, stretched luxuriously and forsook her place in the chair to come and sniff at Merlin's ankles.

"Hypnosis is induced by suggesting sleep," read Merlin.

Mittens leaped to the top of the desk and engaged in a careful examination of Merlin's ink bottle.

"Suggest slow, deep breathing. Suggest that the limbs feel heavy and the eyes feel tired. That the eyes become so tired that it is almost impossible to keep them open."

Mittens rubbed his head on Merlin's hand.

"What's up, kitty? You want to go out?"

Merlin went to the door and opened it. Mittens scampered across his toes and down the stairs. Merlin followed to hold open the front door. Mittens scooted past and disappeared in the general direction of the apple tree in the side yard.

Merlin closed the door and examined himself in the hall mirror. He looked deeply into his own eyes. "You are sleepy," he told his image. "Your eyes are heavy . . . so heavy that you cannot keep them open."

Merlin's eyelids were beginning to droop when he was jolted back to full wakefulness by a hideous scream from the side garden. A dog barked angrily.

Merlin snatched open the front door and ran across the porch and around the house. "Get out!" he yelled. "Go on, beat it. Shoo!"

A shaggy yellow mongrel backed away from Mrs. Schmidt's apple tree. In the crotch of one of the higher branches Mittens mewed plaintively.

"Scat, dog!" Merlin stamped his foot. "Git! Go on!"

The dog loped away.

Merlin walked to the apple tree and looked up at

Mittens. "All right," he said, "you can come down now."

The cat only huddled closer to the tree trunk.

"He's gone," reassured Merlin. "There's nothing to be afraid of."

Mittens stayed put.

Merlin shook a finger at the cat. "You have to stop being such a scared cat," he scolded. "Why don't you stand up to that dog just once?"

Mittens had the grace to look embarrassed.

"What are you, a cat or a mouse?" Merlin demanded.

Mittens didn't seem to know.

At that instant Merlin had one of his greater ideas. "Mittens," he said firmly. "You are about to be my first experiment in helpful hypnosis."

Mittens was unmoved.

Merlin gestured. "You are relaxed," he told the cat. "You are very, very relaxed—and sleepy. Very sleepy. Your eyes are becoming so heavy you can hardly keep them open."

A glazed look stole over Mittens' eyes. Her lids twitched.

"You will fall into a deep, hypnotic sleep," commanded Merlin. "Close your eyes."

The cat's eyes closed.

"You are now in a hypnotic trance," said Merlin.
The cat remained still, apparently sound asleep.

"You are a member of a noble family," said Merlin.
His voice was stronger now, filled with rising excitement. "You are cousin to the leopard and the tiger. You are cousin to the king of beasts himself—the mighty lion! From now on there will be no more running away like a frightened mouse. You will face your enemies like a tiger! You will roar like a lion! Now, when I say three, you will awake, mighty Mittens!"

Merlin stepped back out of the way. "One! Two! Three!" he counted.

Mittens' eyes opened. As Merlin watched, the cat seemed to swell and grow larger. Mittens opened her mouth and roared. It was a deep, rumbling, earth-shaking roar. The fiercest lion ever to prowl the veld would have been proud of that roar. Then Mittens flashed down from the tree and streaked for the corner of the house. The cousin of the leopard and the tiger was after her prey!

Merlin was not quite quick enough to see the entire

encounter between Mittens and the dog. He heard Mittens roar once more. There was an anguished, high-pitched yelp from the dog, followed by the sound of boxes falling. Merlin arrived in the backyard in time to see the dog scrambling desperately onto a pile of old cartons near the fence. Mittens was behind, but closing in fast.

"Wait a minute!" cried Merlin.

The dog dropped from sight behind the fence.

"Here, kitty, kitty, kitty," called Merlin.

Mittens gained the top of the fence and disappeared.

"You're overdoing it," warned Merlin. He looked over the fence. Somehow the dog had managed to get himself up into a tree. At the base of the tree sat Mittens, daintily washing her ear with her paw.

"Well, I'll be doggoned," said Merlin. "It worked!"

Behind Merlin, a window went up. "Merlin, is that you?" called Mrs. Schmidt.

"Yes, it is."

"What was all that noise?"

"Mittens chased that old yellow dog up a tree."

"Oh! I'm so glad. Don't forget to lock the door when you come in."

"I won't forget, Mrs. Schmidt."

"Good night, Merlin."

"Good night, Mrs. Schmidt."

Merlin was up early the next morning—very early. The sun was just creeping up behind the athletic field when he braked the blue convertible to a stop in front of the science building. No other cars were in sight. Merlin grinned with satisfaction. He had beaten Norman to the psych lab.

Inside the lab, Stanley the chimpanzee was dully staring at his own toes. Stanley did not look like a healthy chimp. He looked, in fact, like a chimp with things on his mind—unhappy things.

"Poor Stanley," said Merlin.

Stanley regarded Merlin with some apprehension and moved cautiously back away from the bars of his cage.

"I wouldn't hurt you, Stanley," murmured Merlin. "I want you to know that I don't like the way Norman treats you."

Stanley started staring at his toes again.

"You have rights, too," said Merlin. "He acts like

you're a prisoner. He never gives you any affection or understanding."

Stanley nodded. It was true.

"Stanley, I want you to pay close attention to what I say." Merlin's tone was brisk now, and commanding. Stanley hitched forward and looked up into Merlin's face.

"I want to help you," said Merlin. "I think I can." He held up one finger and began to move it slowly back and forth in front of the chimpanzee. Stanley's head swayed as he followed the movement from side to side.

"You're tired," Merlin told the chimp. "You're very tired. Your eyes are heavy . . . heavy. You can hardly keep them open."

The chimp blinked, but continued to stare at Merlin's finger.

"Your eyes are closing. When I count three you will fall into a deep, deep sleep. One! Two! Three!"

The chimp's eyes closed.

"You are now in a hypnotic trance," said Merlin. "Open your eyes."

Stanley obeyed.

"Your people have made great contributions to

science," Merlin said earnestly. "No one has a prouder record in the conquest of space. But you have accepted Norman's low opinion of you. You have bowed to his tyranny. I intend to liberate you from that."

Merlin swung the cage door open. "Come out, Stanley."

Even in a hypnotic trance, Stanley was afraid. He hung back.

"Come on, Stanley." Merlin was firm.

The chimp came timidly out of the cage. Merlin pointed to the chair pulled up before a big desk. Norman customarily sat there when he was in the lab. Still bashful, Stanley climbed onto the chair and huddled there.

"Sit up like a man," said Merlin.

Stanley straightened himself in the chair.

"You're just as good as Norman," said Merlin. "Maybe you're better. Remember how you finished Professor Shattuck's psychological test before Norman did?"

Stanley grinned, showing a vast expanse of white teeth.

"You have rights, and you have to stand up for

them," Merlin declared. "Don't let Norman push you around anymore."

The chimpanzee seemed to understand. He grinned again and clapped his hands enthusiastically.

"Atta boy!" applauded Merlin.

The door at the top of the stairs banged open, then slammed again. "Get out of my chair!" shouted Norman.

Stanley squealed and began to run for his cage, but he caught Merlin's eye in time. Merlin shook his head and Stanley resumed his seat at Norman's desk.

Norman galloped down the stairs two at a time. "I said get out of my chair!" he bellowed.

Stanley stayed put.

Norman turned on Merlin. "I warned you about that monkey, Jones!" he yelled.

"Chimpanzee," corrected Merlin. "What's the matter? I haven't been feeding him bananas."

Norman turned back to Stanley. "You get right in that cage!" he ordered.

Defiant, Stanley folded his arms across his chest.

"You see! You spoiled the monkey!"

"Chimp!" insisted Merlin.

"Now I'm going to *un*-spoil him!" Norman picked up a yardstick and advanced on Stanley.

"Norman! You wouldn't dare!" cried Merlin. "Now calm down. Let's talk this whole thing over—man to man to chimp!"

But Norman pushed Merlin aside and continued his deliberate, menacing approach toward Stanley.

Merlin grabbed at the yardstick and Norman swung around, one huge fist raised. "Let go, Jones, or I'll slug you!" he threatened.

Now Stanley waded in to prove that he had indeed profited by Merlin's hypnotic instruction. He gave Norman a resounding slap full on the side of the head.

The big athlete reeled, colliding with a cabinet that was crammed with small bottles and vials. The cabinet went over with a crash, taking Norman with it.

Excited by the noise, Stanley leaped to the top of a bookcase and commenced pelting the fallen Norman with the heaviest volumes he could lay hand to.

"Stanley, stop!" pleaded Merlin. "Come down from there."

Norman scrambled to his feet just in time to get a copy of Brooks's *Psychology of the Upper Vertebrates* right on the nose. He fell back, jarring the wall. On a high shelf above Norman's head, a five-gallon glass jug of antiseptic green soap teetered, rocked back and forth, then fell and shattered on Norman's head.

Stanley danced gleefully atop the bookcase, clasping his hands over his head like a small prizefighter.

"Oh, Stanley, please get back in your cage." Merlin knelt beside Norman. The football hero was completely unconscious, and so thoroughly slippery with green soap that Merlin could hardly pull him upright. He succeeded at last, gripping him by the shirt front, in getting Norman to a sitting position and rolling the desk chair behind him to support his back.

"Back in the cage," muttered Norman, beginning to come around. He blinked at Merlin like a myopic owl.

"It's me, Norman," said Merlin. "Not Stanley."

Norman winced and felt a tender place on his head. "You're in trouble, Jones," he said sourly. "You attacked me with a deadly weapon."

"Me?" Merlin was astounded. Then he looked down and realized that, unwittingly, he had picked up the neck of the broken soap bottle.

Stanley danced merrily in and pushed at the chair

that had been supporting Norman.

"Stanley!" cried Merlin.

But it was too late. Norman fell back. His head hit the floor and he lapsed again into unconsciousness. Losing his courage at last, Stanley fled to his cage and pulled the door closed behind him.

At this, the worst of all possible times, Officer Caedmon P. Lightfoot appeared at the top of the stairs. One glance told him all he had to know. There was the lab— a wilderness of broken glass and torn books. There was Norman, unconscious and bleeding, lying in a sticky green pool. And there was Merlin, the incriminating broken bottle still clutched in his hand.

"I got a call to handle a riot," Caddy said grimly. "I should have known you were it, Jones!"

5

Officer Caedmon P. Lightfoot was in his glory, testifying before Judge Holmsby.

"At seven ten this morning, a call came into police headquarters," said Caddy in his most official manner. "The caller was the night watchman at Midvale College. He explained that he was just going off duty and he wanted to report a disturbance in the basement of the science building. He said it sounded like a riot was going on down there."

"Then he had not investigated the cause of the disturbance himself?" asked Judge Holmsby.

"No, your Honor. He said it wasn't on his shift, so someone else should check into it. Like I said, he was going off duty."

"He sounds terribly conscientious," remarked the judge. "Do go on, Officer Lightfoot."

"I was dispatched to the college," said Caddy. "I arrived at seven twenty exactly."

"And what did you find?"

"Oh, there was a riot all right." Caddy was very positive.

"Officer Lightfoot!" The judge's voice cut like a knife. "Be more specific," he instructed. "The dictionary defines a riot as a tumultuous disturbance involving three or more persons. Was there, in fact, a riot at the college?"

Caddy looked dashed. "Oh? Well, I guess you couldn't really call it a riot, then, your Honor. There were only two persons—Merlin Jones and that big fellow there, Norman Powell." Caddy pointed to the table in front of the courtroom where Norman sat, a fresh bandage concealing the bump on his head. Norman had washed up and changed his clothes, but traces of green soap still lingered in his ears and under his fingernails. At another table, Merlin listened attentively to the testimony.

"They were in the basement room where the animals are kept," Caddy continued. "The big guy—Mr. Powell —was stretched out cold on the floor. Jones was kneeling over him with a hunk of broken bottle in his hand. The place was a mess; there was glass everywhere."

"I see. Thank you, Officer Lightfoot."

Caddy subsided into a chair next to Merlin, and Judge Holmsby turned his attention to the broken soap bottle, which rested on his desk. "An ugly weapon!" he said. "Mr. Powell?"

Norman stood up.

"Mr. Jones has appeared before this court several times in the past," said the judge, "but never for assault. I do not understand why he would attack you so viciously."

"Because I wouldn't let him spoil the monkey," explained Norman.

"I object," cried Merlin.

Judge Holmsby attempted to squelch this outburst. "This is an informal hearing, Mr. Jones," he told Merlin. "You'll have a chance to answer the charges against you, but in the meantime there's no point in raising procedural objections to the accusations, because—"

"I'm not objecting to the accusation," said Merlin. "You're not?"

"No, sir. I'm objecting to his calling the chimpanzee a monkey. Monkeys are long-tailed primates of the families *Cebidae, Callitrichidae, or Cercopithecidae.*

But the chimpanzee is the highest of the anthropoid or manlike apes. Chimpanzees have no tails, and—"

The judge rapped with his pencil. "Enough," he said. "You've made your point. It's a chimpanzee, not a monkey."

"That's the trouble, Judge," Norman put in. "He thinks that ape is something special. He keeps spoiling him."

"And you bully him!" Merlin accused.

The judge was more than interested in this last statement. "Is that why you attacked this young man?" he asked Merlin.

"No, sir. I didn't attack him."

Judge Holmsby picked up the broken bottle and held it gingerly toward Merlin. "You did not hit him on the head with this object?"

"No, sir."

"Did he hit himself on the head with it?"

"No, sir." Merlin smiled in spite of himself. "The bottle fell on him," he explained. "It was standing on a high shelf and when Norman fell against the wall it was shaken loose."

The judge put the bottle down. "Did you strike him

or push him?" he asked. "Did you do anything to cause him to fall against the wall?"

Merlin hesitated a moment, then, "No, sir," he said.

"Well, who did?" snapped the judge.

Merlin kept silent.

"Answer my question!" A red flush was creeping up from Holmsby's collar.

Still Merlin remained silent.

"Your Honor, may I have a word?" Professor Shattuck, who had been slouched, unnoticed, in the spectator's section of the courtroom, came forward.

"Yes, Professor?"

"Your Honor," Shattuck said firmly, "it is true that I was at home having breakfast when all this happened, but I do know that Merlin Jones did not willfully cause harm to Norman Powell."

"Oh?" The judge was puzzled. "How do you know this if, as you say, you were home having breakfast when the event in question took place?"

"It's a simple matter of psychology," explained Shattuck. "Violence is not part of Merlin's character. Psychologically speaking, it would be unsound to believe that he ever—"

The judge's pencil drummed sharply on the desk. "I am sure that, psychologically speaking, he is an admirable young man," said Holmsby caustically. "However, it is still necessary for us to discover what happened in the basement of the science building this morning."

He turned to Merlin. "I can compel you to answer," he warned. "You can save all of us a lot of time if you tell me right now."

In the spectators' section, a second champion rose to speak for Merlin. "Can't you see that he's protecting someone?" cried Jennifer.

"Oh, dear!" moaned Judge Holmsby. "It's our young friend of the court!" He beckoned Jennifer forward. "Very well, miss, we seem to be having open forum here today. What have you to say?"

The judge's manner was forbidding, and Jen hesitated a moment.

"Don't tell me *you* did it?" said the judge.

"No, your Honor, not me. The chimp."

"The chimp!" Holmsby's bewilderment was complete.

"At first I thought it was Merlin, too," said Jen. "But it couldn't be. He just isn't that kind of a person."

"Is this true, Mr. Jones?" demanded the judge.

"Yes, sir," Merlin admitted. "It is true that the chimpanzee struck the blow, but I'm the one responsible. The chimp acted under my influence."

"You mean you trained the animal to attack its keeper?"

"Oh, no, sir." Merlin was shocked at the very idea. "But I did tell Stanley—"

"Stanley?"

"The chimpanzee. I told him to stand up for his rights, and I guess he got carried away."

"You *told* him?" The judge had a feeling that he had wandered into a particularly puzzling dream. "You *told* an animal to stand up for his rights?"

"I hypnotized him," said Merlin. "I've been making a study of hypnotic suggestion. I tried it out on my landlady's cat and changed her whole personality."

"The landlady's?" asked Holmsby.

"No, sir. The cat's."

Judge Holmsby took out a large white handkerchief and wiped his brow. "And just what did you plan to do with this ape's personality?" he asked.

"There are endless possibilities," said Merlin. "Did

you know that a chimp has the same ridges in his brain that you have?"

"How would you like to be cited for contempt of court?" was Holmsby's icy rejoinder.

"I don't mean you personally," Merlin hastened to explain. "I mean his brain ridges are the same as man's. I want Stanley to realize his full potentialities."

"Talk about crackpot ideas," sneered Norman.

"All ideas are crackpot until they're perfected," Merlin countered.

Norman grimaced. "I can't stand smart animals," he said finally.

"I know," Merlin replied.

The judge deliberated for a minute. "You went to the psych lab simply because you wanted to hypnotize that chimpanzee?" he asked Merlin.

"Yes, sir."

He turned to Norman. "And you're in charge of the chimp?"

"Yes, sir."

The judge rubbed his chin. "It doesn't appear to me that Mr. Jones had any intent to harm you," he pointed out. "Under the circumstances, I don't feel there is any cause for action against him."

Merlin's face lighted with a smile of triumph, but it quickly faded as the judge went on speaking.

"Mr. Jones," instructed Judge Holmsby, "in all fairness to Mr. Powell, I must order you to stay away from that chimpanzee from now on. Is that clear?"

Merlin nodded.

"That's all," said Judge Holmsby. "And, Mr. Jones. . . ."

"Yes, sir?"

"I do hope you'll not be back here in my courtroom." The judge spoke with heartfelt warmth.

"No, sir," said Merlin dispiritedly.

Professor Shattuck and Jennifer waited until they were out of the courtroom before they congratulated Merlin.

"You were lucky today," Shattuck told him. "It could have turned out pretty badly for you."

"I know," Merlin agreed. "I messed up everything. I wanted to help Stanley, and all I did was get in trouble. Now I can't even go near Stanley."

"Oh, come on, Merlin. Cheer up." Professor Shattuck patted Merlin on the back. "You worry about the chimp too much. I'm sure Stanley's okay."

"He's not okay. Norman hates him."

Shattuck stopped at the courthouse door and looked searchingly at Merlin. "I'll admit that Norman isn't exactly fond of Stanley," he said, "but that really isn't any of your business. Norman is the student aide in charge of the lab animals. As long as he feeds them and keeps them clean, he's doing his job. I don't feel I can ask him to love them."

"But he bullies the chimp," protested Merlin.

"Do you mean that he mistreats Stanley?" asked the professor. "If he does, he should be removed. But you'd have to prove a thing like that to the dean, and I don't think you have any proof, do you?".

Merlin remembered Norman threatening the chimpanzee with the yardstick, but he realized immediately that Norman could plead unusual and extenuating circumstances. After all, Merlin *had* let the chimp out of his cage.

"Forget it," advised Professor Shattuck. "I promise you, I'll keep an eye on Stanley. Now I've got to get back to school. I've got a class at eleven. Can I give either of you a lift?"

"No, thanks, Professor. I'm just going over to the Campus Cafe for the noon shift."

"I'll tag along with Merlin," Jen volunteered. "I missed breakfast and I could use a sandwich."

"You'll have to walk," warned Merlin. "My car's still in front of the science building."

"That's okay," Jen insisted.

The professor waved and loped across the parking lot to his car, an ancient, shabbily respectable gray sedan.

"He's a good guy," Merlin remarked, "but I think he's all wet about Norman."

Jennifer started down the courthouse steps. "He's only trying to be fair," she said. "You can't expect him to fire Norman without some awfully good reason."

"I guess not. And Norman does get along like a house afire with the rats and the hamsters. It's only Stanley who bothers him. You heard him today; he hates smart animals."

"So?"

"So maybe the thing to do is to get Stanley out of that lab and away from Norman."

"Out of the lab? Where?"

Merlin shrugged. "I don't know. I'll have to give it

a good think. But he's much too smart to keep in a cage with no company but a bunch of squeaking hamsters."

"And Norman," reminded Jen.

"And Norman," agreed Merlin. He took Jen's arm and steered her down the street toward the town square. "If I could just prove how smart Stanley really is," he said, "maybe I could get Professor Shattuck to make some other arrangements for him."

"Merlin, why are you so sure Stanley is that clever?"

"Oh, he is, Jen. You should have seen the way he responded to my hypnotic commands. He understood every word I said. He was almost human!"

Jen and Merlin walked on in silence for a few minutes. Then Jen said, "But how are you going to prove he's that smart if you can't go near him?"

"It's a problem," Merlin admitted. "I might work out some method for qualitative analysis, and then get the professor to run some tests on Stanley."

"What kind of analysis?"

"Qualitative. I need to find some way to measure his brainpower."

"Merlin, that's silly."

"No, it's not. Haven't you ever heard of an electro-encephalograph?"

"Frankly, no. I haven't."

"It's a device for measuring the alpha waves—the brain waves that appear when the mind is at rest. These waves are blocked out when a person concentrates, so that wouldn't do for what I have in mind. Just the same. . . ."

Merlin stopped dead and studied a crack in the sidewalk with intense concentration.

"Just the same, what?" asked the patient Jennifer.

"Just the same, the principle might be adapted," Merlin said at last. "Listen, Jen, suppose I had a device—like the electroencephalograph—but one that would show the electrical energy put out by a brain at work. And suppose Professor Shattuck used it to measure Stanley's brainpower? I'm sure that a machine like that would prove that Stanley is really a superior animal. Say, Jen, maybe we can get him out of that cage after all—and away from Norman's browbeating!"

"Maybe," agreed Jennifer. "But there's a catch."

"What's that?"

"Where are you going to get the electro—electro—

the thing to measure brainpower?"

Merlin was undaunted. "I'll build one," he declared. "I'll work out an adaptation of the standard device. And by the way, I thought you were hungry."

"I'm starved."

"Well, let's go. We'll get you a table at the Campus Cafe before the lunch crowd descends."

But at the cafe, Merlin and Jennifer quickly forgot all about food. Effie, the waitress, heard them come in. She opened the kitchen door and called, "Merlin, your landlady phoned. She asked if you could come home for a minute."

"What's the matter, Effie?" Merlin asked.

"Something about her cat," said Effie. "I couldn't quite get the whole thing. There was some kind of noise on the wire. It sounded like she said the cat chased the mailman up a tree, but of course it couldn't be that."

Merlin sighed. "Effie," he said sadly, "that's just what it probably is."

It took Merlin twenty minutes to convince Mittens that, while yellow mongrel dogs might actually *need* to be chased once in awhile, humans—and particularly mailmen—should be treated with respect by any cousin of the lordly lion. Mittens retreated under Mrs. Schmidt's front porch to think this over, and the mailman climbed down from his tree and went his way— after sternly warning Mrs. Schmidt that she had better keep her cat under control in the future, or she'd have to come to the post office to get her mail.

Merlin left Mrs. Schmidt, who seemed inclined to the viewpoint that the mailman had somehow insulted Mittens, and hurried back to the Campus Cafe. Jennifer was gone. Her corner table was occupied by a pair of stout ladies who were enjoying the diet special—with extra mayonnaise.

"Hurry up, Merlin!" Effie urged. "You're late and we're running behind."

Merlin hurried, deftly pouring coffee, filling water glasses, and carrying orders into and laden trays out of the kitchen. By one thirty the last of the lunch crowd had taken the last sip of coffee, deposited the last dimes under the edge of the saucer, and wandered off to face whatever the afternoon would bring. Merlin was free to get to work on his project. He grabbed a quick malt and headed for the campus.

In a small and painfully neat office on the third floor of the science building, Merlin found Dr. Faraday, head of the physics department. Faraday was engaged in the painful task of marking test papers.

"Excuse me, sir." Merlin rapped on the panels of the open door.

Faraday had just come to a paper in which a student described kinetic energy as a type of extreme nervousness. He was happy for any interruption. He put down his red pencil and nodded Merlin toward a chair.

"I wanted to ask a favor, Dr. Faraday," Merlin began. "I'd like permission to use a corner of the physics lab for an experiment."

"Oh?" Faraday's left eyebrow shot up. "Is this an assignment?" he asked.

"No, sir. It's a private project. I've got a theory I want to test, and I'll have to devise some apparatus."

Faraday grunted. "Well, at least you have a theory," he said. "Most of the students at Midvale wouldn't know a theory if it walked up and clutched them around the neck. What's involved in this experiment of yours?"

"Some electrical supplies. I can buy them easily."

"Very well. There's just one thing, Jones. Your uncle had a private experiment going once, in the chemistry lab, and. . . ."

Merlin held up his hand. "Nothing will explode," he promised.

"You're sure?"

"Positive. No explosives at all. Just a device to measure electrical impulses."

"Sounds safe enough. All right, the two tables next to the windows in the lab aren't used much. You can have that space."

"Thank you, sir." Merlin rose.

"And Jones!"

Merlin stopped in the doorway.

"Be careful!" warned Dr. Faraday.

With his lab space assured, Merlin hurried to gather

up the materials he would need. Jennifer helped him shop for miles of fine copper wiring, insulators, tubes, rolls of graph paper, and, finally, a football helmet.

Thus equipped, Merlin shut himself up in the physics lab, and for nearly two weeks Jen saw little of him. He appeared at her house every morning promptly at eight, and he drove her home every afternoon, but he hardly spoke to her. And between times he was in class, at the cafe, or in the lab.

Jennifer, knowing he had problems to work out, held her peace until the afternoon he failed to appear to drive her home. Increasingly impatient, she waited in the parking lot next to the science building while three thirty crept toward four, and four became four twenty.

Norman Powell, on his way to the psych lab, stopped beside the blue convertible and favored her with a truly hideous grin. "What's the matter, doll baby?" he asked. "You get stood up?"

Jennifer turned her back on him.

Norman waited a moment, then decided that there must have been something wrong with his first approach. He began again. "Jen, the Lettermen's

Ball is next Saturday. It'll be the swingin'est deal of the year!"

"Sorry, Norman, I have a date."

"With Merlin Jones?"

Jen said nothing.

"You're off your rocker goin' with a kook like that," said Norman bitterly.

"Norman, isn't it about time you fed the animals in the lab?" Jen hurried off and ran up the steps into the science building. Angered and humiliated by her encounter with Norman, she sped to the physics lab. "Merlin Jones!" she cried, bursting in. "You were supposed to meet me an hour ago!"

Merlin looked around calmly. "Oh, hi, Jen."

"You're just sitting there, reading a newspaper," Jen accused. "And what's that thing on your head?"

Jennifer hardly recognized the football helmet that Merlin wore. It was completely covered with wire coils and insulators. Antennae shot up in every direction. The helmet was now fitted with two earphones, from which wires looped down to connect with what appeared to be a plywood box. Knobs and flashing lights covered one side of the box while on top of it an automatic pen made squiggly lines on a slowly unrolling sheet of graph paper.

"I'm not just reading," said Merlin.

"It sure looks as if you are," countered Jen. "I've been standing down there in the parking lot all afternoon."

Merlin was instantly contrite. "I'm sorry, Jennie. I forgot the time. But I think I'm really getting somewhere with this. Look!" Excited, he urged Jen to watch the lines being traced on the graph. "It's supersensitive," he declared. "It records the brain waves put out by *any* mental activity!"

"That's fascinating!" said Jennifer, who didn't think it was fascinating at all. "But you were supposed to meet me—"

"Let's dance," suggested Merlin.

"Merlin, will you be serious?"

"I am serious." He adjusted a knob on his device and flipped a switch. The machine gave forth a rhythmic "beep . . . beep . . . beep."

"Even an activity like dancing must have a distinctive brain wave pattern," he explained.

"But I'm supposed to get home!" Jennifer protested.

"Oh, all right." Merlin reluctantly took off the helmet. "Just help me get this stuff in the car," he said.

"In the car?"

"Sure. I'll be hooked into the system while I drive. We'll see what the machine comes up with then."

"Merlin, that's ridiculous."

"Scientific experiments always seem ridiculous at first. Just remember, Jen, this is all for a good cause."

"I know," said Jennifer wearily. "Stanley!"

"That's right. And not only Stanley." Merlin handed the helmet to Jennifer and picked up the plywood box which served as console for his strange device. "This gadget could benefit everybody. Take bad drivers, for instance—the ones that are always having accidents. With this super-electroencephalograph, you could probably find out why. Maybe they don't pay attention. Maybe they're always worried or upset."

"Maybe my mother'll have a fit if I don't get home soon." suggested Jen.

"Then let's go!"

In the car Jen held the console on her lap while Merlin donned the helmet.

"Now watch the graph," Merlin instructed.

"I will," Jen said obediently.

Merlin pulled carefully out of the parking lot. "What's it doing?" he asked.

"Making a little wavery line," answered Jennifer.

The blue convertible rolled through the college gates. At the intersection of North and Sixteenth, a ball bounced into the road. Merlin stamped on the brake just in time to miss a small boy who darted out after the ball. The stylus on the graph danced in excited arcs. "Wow!" commented Jen. "Got a bit wild there."

In front of the Campus Cafe, the pen jiggled suddenly. "I forgot to fill the sugar bowls this noon," said Merlin.

"No need to get that upset about it," Jen replied.

Merlin glanced over at the graph. "Jen, it's working beautifully!"

"It sure is. But what's that funny noise?" The low-pitched hum of the machine was drowned out by a slowly rising whine.

Merlin put his hand up to the helmet and frowned. "That's a new one. Could something be happening to my brain?"

On the graph the pen leaped in ever-widening arcs.

"The vibrations are getting bigger and bigger," said Jen. "You're practically off the tape."

The high whine slid down the scale to die in a moan. Merlin glanced to his left. "Uh-oh!" he said.

Caddy Lightfoot, having at last succeeded in getting Merlin's attention, killed the siren on his motorcycle and waved the blue convertible to the curb. Caddy parked his motorcycle with exquisite care. He was pulling his book from his pocket as he strolled around to Merlin's side of the car.

"Let me see your license," he said.

Merlin produced his license.

"When are you going to learn you can't fool around in traffic?" Caddy began to write a ticket.

"But we weren't fooling around," said Merlin.

Caddy shot a withering glare at Merlin. "Those wires grow out of your head, I suppose?"

"No, sir, it—"

"It's part of a scientific experiment," Jen put in.

Merlin touched an antenna. "This is a modification of the basic principle of the electroencephalograph," he explained. "These electrodes will pick up—"

"Knock it off, college boy," interrupted Caddy. "You

want to go around disguised as a grasshopper, you wait for Halloween. Sign the ticket."

"You mean you won't even let him explain?" Jennifer was indignant.

"I've heard his explanations before." Caddy held his book toward Merlin. "Just sign," he ordered.

"Don't do it!" snapped Jen.

"Huh?" Merlin, resigned to his fate, already had Caddy's pencil in his hand.

"Don't sign unless you have a chance to explain," Jennifer insisted.

Merlin handed the pencil back to Caddy.

"All right." Caddy tore off the unsigned ticket and gave it to Merlin. "You'll get your chance to explain, and so will the young lady. You can tell it to Judge Holmsby!"

"Oh, no!" groaned Jennifer.

Caddy stepped back and saluted them. "See you tomorrow," he said cheerfully. "Usual time—usual place: ten o'clock, at the courthouse!"

Jennifer's thought, the next morning, was that she and Merlin should enter Judge Holmsby's courtroom in a very, very inconspicuous manner. She soon found, however, that it is completely impossible to be inconspicuous while carrying an experimental, supersensitive electroencephalograph. A bailiff stared at them when they tried to tiptoe into the back of the courtroom. Several spectators turned around to gape and giggle. Jennifer and Merlin found seats in the very back row and tried to blend into the wood paneling.

Judge Holmsby, letting his eyes roam over the courtroom, discovered Merlin crouched behind his tangle of electrical gear. "Good heavens!" said the judge. He beckoned to the clerk. "Are we, by any chance, hearing a case involving a Merlin Jones this morning?"

The clerk nodded and handed a paper up to the judge. "Merlin Jones!" he cried.

Merlin and Jen struggled to their feet and started toward the bench. Merlin carried the console while Jen trailed behind with the football helmet.

"My sainted aunt!" murmured the judge. Then, louder, he said, "Just put that—that—whatever it is on the table, Mr. Jones."

Jennifer and Merlin deposited their burdens on the table in front of the bench and waited while Judge

Holmsby, with fierce deliberation, poured himself a glass of water and drank it. Next the judge set the empty glass on the tray at one side of his desk, patted his lips carefully with his handkerchief, and then he clasped his hands and looked at Merlin in silence for quite a few minutes. Merlin found himself turning red under this judicial scrutiny. He had to restrain the impulse to look at the floor and shuffle his feet.

At last Judge Holmsby spoke. "I am sure you will agree, Mr. Jones, that your appearances in this courtroom have been, er, rather out of the ordinary."

"Yes, sir."

"They have also been far too frequent!"

"Yes, sir."

"Now, why are you here on this particular morning?"

The clerk read the charge—reckless driving—and Caddy announced that Merlin's attitude had been uncooperative. He had refused to sign the ticket.

"He just wanted a chance to explain," cried Jen.

"He is getting his chance," snapped the judge. "Mr. Jones?"

"I wasn't driving recklessly," said Merlin. "I was

driving with care and complete concentration. I had to, or the experiment would have been worthless."

"A-ha!" said the judge. "Another experiment?"

"Yes, sir." Merlin picked up the helmet and put it on. "This device uses the basic principle of the electro-encephalograph," he began, plugging himself into the console.

He turned dials and flicked a switch. A soft "blip . . . blip . . . blip" came from the machine.

"I've been recording the various patterns made by the electrical energy given off by the brain during various mental activities. The alpha waves, the brain waves shown on the conventional encephalogram, appear when the mind is at rest. But, as you can see, I've been able to record the electrical energy given off during concentrated mental activity."

"Such as driving in traffic," said Jen brightly.

The judge was aghast. "Young man, do I under-stand that you were driving with that thing on your head?"

"Well, of course, your Honor. How else could I—"

The judge slapped the desk with the flat of his hand. "This is outrageous!" he exploded. "I have spoken to you before on this subject. Your experiments must be conducted in a laboratory, and not while driving a car. Driving demands your entire concentration."

"But that's just the point, sir. I have to drive with full concentration or I won't get the reading I want."

"That's enough!" stormed the judge. "You are *not* to continue this experiment—or any experiment—in traffic. Is that clear?"

Jennifer, upset by his tone, lost all caution. "That's interference with the freedom of scientific inquiry," she cried.

The judge looked at her for a moment, then he turned back to Merlin. "Last spring you were charged with unauthorized use of a siren," he said.

"But that wasn't really a siren," Merlin pointed out.

"We will not go into it again," said the judge. "A few weeks ago you created an uproar in the town square when your car spewed forth clouds of green exhaust. I am afraid I will have to impress upon you the serious responsibility attached to the deadly weapon called the automobile. I am going to suspend your license for ten days!"

Merlin gulped.

"Surrender your license to the clerk!" commanded the judge.

Merlin sadly took off the football helmet and handed over his license. Jen helped him gather up his equipment. As they turned to leave the court, Jen was suddenly overwhelmed by the severity of the sentence.

"I think that was uncalled for," she flung at the bench. "Also unfair and probably unconstitutional!"

"That will do, young lady," warned Judge Holmsby. "One more word and you will be cited for contempt!"

Jen subsided and let Merlin hurry her out of the room.

"Well, back to the lab," said Merlin unhappily when they had gained the safety of the courthouse corridor.

"Never mind, Merlin. Ten days isn't forever, and I can drive you wherever you want to go."

"You're great, Jen."

Jen thought of the exchange she had just had with Judge Holmsby. "I'm real great!" she agreed. "With a friend like me, you'll go far, Merlin Jones—like maybe to Sing Sing!"

7   THE HIGH-VOLTAGE BRAIN

Dr. Faraday came quietly up the steps of the science building and went into the physics lab. He was looking particularly well-polished and he sported a carnation in the lapel of his dark blue suit.

The lights were on in the lab. At a table in the corner, Merlin Jones, wearing his electronic helmet, worked overtime at his rows of dials and knobs and switches.

"Merlin," called Dr. Faraday, "have you seen my briefcase?"

"Isn't it in your office?" asked Merlin, without looking up.

"No, it isn't. And you're working too close to that electrical control panel. Take that thing off your head and move. . . ."

Merlin turned, too suddenly. A wire from his helmet swung into contact with the electrical panel. A blue arc leaped from Merlin's helmet to the control board. The lights went out. There was a crackling noise and sparks showered around Merlin's shoulders. With small popping explosions, several tubes on the console burst.

"Turn the switch off!" shouted Faraday.

"I can't!" Merlin sounded as if he were strangling. "I can't move!"

"The master switch!" Stumbling in the darkened lab, Faraday somehow got to the door. Outside he found, and pulled, the switch that controlled all the current for the building.

"Merlin! Are you all right?" The lab was now completely black.

"I . . . think . . . so." Merlin's voice was shaky.

Faraday struck a match and, after some fumbling, found a candle stub in a cupboard.

"No burns or anything?" With the candle in one hand, he hastily helped Merlin disconnect himself.

"No, sir. I'm okay."

"It's a miracle," gasped Faraday. "You could have been killed." He pulled a high laboratory stool over and forced Merlin to sit down. "Stay here," he ordered. "I'll take care of the lights."

By the time Dr. Faraday had replaced numerous

blown fuses in the basement of the building, then thrown the master switch in the hall, Merlin was feeling normal again. Faraday stood in the doorway of the lab and watched him scribbling on a long yellow pad.

Making notes on how it feels to be nearly electrocuted, Faraday said to himself. *I've had some screwy students in my time, but this kid's got them all beat!*

Merlin looked up and smiled. "I'm not really screwy, Dr. Faraday," he said. "I'm just inquisitive."

Faraday's hand flew to his closed lips. *I didn't say it,* he told himself dazedly. *I only thought it.*

"But I heard you," said Merlin.

"There!" This time Faraday spoke aloud. "You did it again!"

"Did what?"

"You heard something I didn't say!"

"But how could I do that?" Merlin asked reasonably.

"I don't know, but you did!"

Merlin's nimble mind groped for an answer to this problem. "Maybe that shock charged my brain," he suggested. "Maybe it charged it in a special way, so I receive the electrical energy given off by your thoughts, convert it into sound energy and—"

Faraday laughed. "You have just broken the world's record for conclusion-jumping," he told Merlin. "That's all wild speculation!"

"Of course it is," Merlin agreed. "But we could set up some experiments and—"

"Not tonight." Faraday was firm. "I'm leaving town for a few days and I have something to take care of before I go."

"Whatever it is, I'll help you with it," Merlin offered. "Then we'd have time for—"

"No. It's something I have to do myself."

I'd rather spend my evening with Miss Cartier than with Merlin Jones, thought Faraday.

Merlin immediately understood why the doctor didn't want to explore his new theory. "I don't blame you," Merlin conceded. "She's very pretty."

"Who is?" Faraday was flustered.

"Miss Cartier. I take her class in Intermediate French."

Faraday's face took on a becoming shade of bright red. "Listen, Jones," he scolded, "whatever this thing is that you have, you'd better be careful how you go around butting into people's thoughts."

"I'm sorry," Merlin apologized.

"People have a right to the privacy of their own minds," Faraday pointed out.

"Sure they do," Merlin agreed.

"You go poking around in people's thoughts with your electrified brain and you'll get in trouble!"

"I'll be careful about that," Merlin promised humbly.

"And another thing," said Faraday. "Don't tell anyone about this."

"Not even Jennifer?" asked Merlin.

Faraday was horrified. "Especially not Jennifer!" he cried. And he left, slamming the door behind him.

Merlin meditated upon this advice and decided that it was probably extremely sound. He put away his notes, checked his console to make sure it was turned off, put out the lab lights, and went out into the brisk October evening. He cut across the athletic field and half ran up the broad stone steps of the college library.

Miss Beck, the assistant librarian, was on duty at the desk in the main reading room.

"I want some books on—" began Merlin.

"Shh!" warned Miss Beck.

Merlin whispered, "I want some books on mind reading."

"Fiction is on the second floor," hissed Miss Beck.

"I don't want fiction. I want scientific material on the electrification of a person's brain so that it becomes sensitized to receive other people's thoughts."

Behind steel-rimmed glasses, Miss Beck's eyes softened. *The poor boy's been studying too hard,* she thought.

Merlin denied this instantly. "No. I'm lucky," he said. "I don't have to study very hard. It comes easy to me."

"What did you say?" asked the astonished librarian.

"Uh—nothing," said Merlin. "I—I meant, I'll just look around for myself."

Merlin retreated to the stacks in the back of the reading room. Prowling through the science section, he caught sight of the title *Transference of Electrical Impulses*. It sounded promising, and he took the book from the shelf.

Merlin Jones, the perfect pigeon!

The voice sounded in Merlin's brain. It was familiar and very close. Merlin removed three more books from the shelf and peeked through the gap. On the other side of the stack was Henry Biggers, the campus moocher.

Merlin Jones! Henry chuckled inwardly. *I can squeeze ten bucks out of him with a sob story anyone else would laugh at.*

Merlin quickly formulated his defense. As Henry came into sight around the end of the bookshelf, Merlin greeted him warmly. Henry smirked. The touch was as good as made. But then Merlin dropped his bombshell.

"Hey, Henry," he said innocently, "can you loan me ten bucks?"

Henry let out a sound that reminded Merlin of a leaky air hose, shook his head, and hurried past. Merlin smiled, filled in the gap in the bookshelf and, carrying *Transference of Electrical Impulses,* made for a seat at one of the long library tables.

Louise Everhart looked up from her solid geometry text as Merlin took a seat at the other end of the table. *Jennifer's lucky,* she mused, pushing back her exceedingly golden hair. *I wish I had someone like Merlin to help me with math.*

Merlin tried not to blush.

He's sort of cute, too, in a weird sort of way.

Merlin stood his book upright, like a rampart, and tried to ignore her.

Man, I dig this swingin' quiet!

The voice that sounded in Merlin's brain was a new one. He peered around the edge of his book at the character who had the chair next to Louise. Merlin recognized him as a freshman, a thin, sallow boy who had gotten himself up in rigid conformance to the code of the beatnik. He wore the standard black turtleneck sweater and faded jeans. His hair was too long, and a scraggly beard wandered over his thin jaw.

A crazy place for grinding out a cool poem, decided the beat one. He licked the end of his pencil and turned to a clean page in his notebook.

> *Clam, in your wet sand pad,*

he began.

> *Too hip for mankind's bread-love,*
> *When the diggers who don't dig*
> *Are bugged by the chowder troubles. . . .*

Chowder troubles? Merlin shook his head and tried to get back into his tome on electrical impulses.

Chowder troubles? The beatnik had obviously hung himself up on the phrase. *Chowder troubles . . . chowder troubles. . . .* Unable to go on, he worried at the two words, chasing them around and around in his head.

Zachary Taylor was the eleventh man to be President of the United States.

Relieved to get away from the chowder troubles for a minute, Merlin turned toward plump Peggy Granley, who sat across from the poetic freshman. Peggy was obviously preparing for Thursday's American History class.

In his inaugural address, she read silently, *Taylor said . . . I'd give anything in the world for a hot fudge sundae!*

Merlin frowned. It seemed unlikely that Taylor, or any other President, had made that statement in the course of an inaugural address.

All hail, Macbeth! At the next table, Henry Biggers boned up on Shakespeare.

All hail, Macbeth! The words rang nobly in Henry's mind. *Macbeth! Macbeth?* The nobility vanished. *MacDonald!* thought Henry. *Ted MacDonald! I can bor-*

row ten from him! But . . . but no. I still owe him twenty.

Merlin shifted around so that his back was toward Henry.

A plus B cubed equals the square of . . . square! The blue chiffon is too square for the fraternity ball. Across from Merlin, Louise Everhart gave up even trying to accommodate her mind to math. *I need something spectacular, like the black velvet,* she decided.

Merlin began to feel a little desperate. He tried putting his hands over his ears.

The chowder troubles . . . the chowder troubles. . . . The beat freshman chewed the end of his pencil.

The legislative and the judicial branches, read Peggy Granley. *Judicial . . . judicial . . juicy. Oh, for a nice juicy piece of cherry pie!*

Merlin tried slouching low in his seat so that his book was higher than his head. It was no use. Fragments of thought crowded in on him.

Jim Dutton? wondered Henry Biggers. *Ed Turner? Maybe the red wool. . . .* It was Louise again.

The chowder troubles . . . the chowder troubles. . . . Individuals whose integrity and character will furnish ample portions of cherry pie....

Mark Spencer? Henry continued the catalog of his acquaintances. *Hal Benson? Harry Gilbert?*

Nobody's seen the green satin....

The chowder troubles....

Dan Miller? No! Ed Davidson?

Cherry pie ... with ice cream!

I'm going to have to buy new shoes....

The chowder troubles....

"QUIET!"

The cry exploded in the silent room.

Only when he found himself on his feet, with Louise, Peggy, Henry, and the bewildered beatnik staring at him did Merlin realize that he had shouted—out loud —in the sacrosanct main reading room of the college library!

Miss Beck shot out from behind her desk and rushed at him. "Shshshsh!" she hissed, like an agitated balloon. Louise giggled, and the beatnik returned to his chowder troubles.

Merlin, shaking with embarrassment, saw Jennifer come into the library. She waved and started toward him, passing Miss Beck en route.

Merlin managed a hoarse whisper. "Jen, I have to get out of here. It's too noisy."

"Too noisy?" Jen glanced around and noticed the slightly malicious sparkle in Louise Everhart's eye and the amused smirk on Peggy's chubby face. It wasn't noisy, but something was certainly up.

"I mean. . . ." Merlin was sweating. "I mean, I have to get home."

Jen nodded. "I'll drive you as soon as I get my book."

Merlin was trailing her toward the stacks when a new thought thrust itself into his reeling brain: *What does a dish like Jennifer see in a meatball like Merlin?*

Merlin turned to face the desk. Norman Powell had come in. *The campus creep,* Norman thought. He strolled nearer and favored Merlin with one of his ugliest smiles. *Pure, one hundred percent creep!*

"Speaking of creeps . . ." whispered Merlin, the instant Norman was within whispering distance.

Norman recoiled. "Who said anything about creeps?"

"I did," Merlin replied. "You are a creep!"

Norman gathered up a handful of Merlin's sweater. "Say that again!" he snarled.

Merlin smiled happily. "Creep!" he said, and shoved

Norman as hard as he could shove.

Jennifer jumped to one side. Norman let go of Merlin's sweater and stumbled backward, colliding with a high bookcase. The case toppled, connecting with the bookcase one row behind it. This set of shelves tilted and fell, connecting in turn with yet another bookcase. Norman, helping the whole thing along, floundered, stumbled, clutched and grabbed at the rain of books and shelves. He came to rest finally, half sitting, half lying against the wall, buried to his clavicle in books.

Miss Beck fairly leaped over her desk. "Rowdiness will not be tolerated in this library!" she shrilled, forgetting for a moment that shrieking was also frowned upon. She scurried to bend over Norman. "You will pick up every one of these books!" she told the flabbergasted football hero. "And you will return each one to its proper place. Do you understand me?"

Merlin didn't wait to hear Norman's answer. Taking Jen's arm, he walked calmly and with dignity toward the door. He didn't start to laugh until he was safely outside again.

8

The stout woman eased off her shoes and studied the menu of the Campus Cafe. *If I have the ground round and cottage cheese,* she thought, *I can afford to eat just part of a serving of cream pie.*

"No one eats just part of a serving," said Merlin kindly. "Ground round and cottage cheese? Yes, ma'am. Coffee black?"

The woman nodded. She was too startled to remember that she always had cream and sugar in her coffee. Merlin took the menu from her and made for the kitchen.

Merlin did not see the Honorable Curtice C. Holmsby come into the cafe, hang his hat and overcoat near the door, and take a place at a small table for two. When Merlin bounced back in from the kitchen, the judge was comfortably settled, studying the menu. Effie, busy at the coffee urn, cast a worried glance from Merlin to Judge Holmsby.

"I'll take care of him, Effie," Merlin volunteered.

"Watch your step," Effie warned.

"If he orders soup, shall I drop it on him?" Merlin teased.

"Merlin Jones! Don't you dare!"

Merlin grinned at Effie, then made his way to the judge's table. He slapped a water glass down in front of the jurist and filled it from a huge pitcher—being careful to splash a little on the paper place mat.

Judge Holmsby, who seldom noticed waiters, cab drivers, or elevator operators, was aware of Merlin only as a white-coated shape next to his chair. "A green salad," ordered the judge. "French dressing, and black coffee."

"Yes, sir." Merlin scribbled on his pad and withdrew. He considered dropping the salad as he served it but quickly gave up the idea. It wouldn't be wise, especially since Merlin had to go back into court in just eight more days to retrieve his driver's license.

When Merlin returned with the salad, Judge Holmsby was examining something which was scribbled on the back of an envelope. Merlin put the salad down carefully on the table.

I'm afraid I have a tiger by the tail, the judge said to himself.

"Coffee now, sir?" asked Merlin.

Unhearing, the judge continued his reverie. *Each crime I commit has to be bigger than the one before,* he thought sadly.

Merlin jumped, and the coffee cup rattled on its saucer.

The bank swindle and the forgery seem mild now, mused Holmsby. *The payroll robbery was the high point of my career. I never thought I would have to top it.*

"Coffee now, sir?" repeated Merlin.

Holmsby came to with a start. "Yes, I'll have my coffee now."

Merlin poured, his hand shaking so that the coffee splashed over into the saucer. The judge made a grimace of distaste and Merlin hurriedly mopped the saucer and wiped off the bottom of the cup.

In the kitchen, Merlin found Effie contentedly cutting pie. "You ever hear of a payroll robbery around here?" Merlin asked.

Effie wiped her knife on a damp towel. "There was

the Acme payroll robbery," she said. "The papers were full of it last summer."

"Who did it?"

Effie shrugged. "Nobody knows. It was one of those perfect crimes—not even a clue. Why?"

"I'll tell you later, if ever." Merlin left to go and hover behind Judge Holmsby's chair.

I've always been able to use my knowledge of law to perfect my crimes and make them successful, the judge was thinking.

And he's the big deal who took away my driver's license, Merlin said to himself.

The judge finished his salad and leaned back in his chair, sipping his coffee. *I don't like to resort to violence,* he thought. He looked around.

"More coffee, sir?" Merlin leaped forward to pour, and the judge murmured his thanks.

If murder is the only way to safeguard the stolen diamonds, then murder it will be!

Completely unstrung, Merlin dropped the coffeepot. It exploded against the floor, drenching the distinguished Judge Holmsby's trouser legs and splashing over his neat black oxfords.

"I'm so sorry." Merlin made futile mopping motions with a napkin.

"Don't be upset, son." Holmsby stood up and took the napkin from Merlin. "Accidents do happen," he said easily. Then he looked at Merlin—really looked at him—for the first time.

"Mr. Jones!"

"Yes, sir," said Merlin miserably.

Judge Holmsby looked down at his wet suit and sopping shoes. "I hope this *was* an accident!" he said.

"It was, sir. Indeed it was!"

"Because an attitude of resentment against the law can only lead you into further trouble," Holmsby warned. He jammed the napkin back into Merlin's hand and stalked toward the desk, where a flustered proprietor refused his money and showered him with apologies.

Hastily shedding his white coat, Merlin ran out through the kitchen.

"Where are you going?" Effie called after him.

"Out!" snapped Merlin.

The six-block walk to the police station cooled Merlin down somewhat. He did not blurt out his story to the

desk sergeant. Instead, remembering countless television dramas, he asked to see a detective. The sergeant obliged by sending him upstairs to a rather dingy room which contained one desk, a telephone, two straight chairs, a water cooler, and a large, bluff man named Lieutenant Hutchins.

Merlin got the interview off to a booming start by announcing that he could identify the man who masterminded the Acme payroll robbery.

Lieutenant Hutchins was interested, but not very. He had run down a hundred tips on the robbery. He was resigned to running down the hundred and first. He picked up the phone and said a few words. A minute later an officer came in carrying a file folder. Merlin's heart sank when he recognized Caddy. Caddy looked curiously at Merlin, but said nothing.

Lieutenant Hutchins put the file to one side, took a pad of paper and a pencil from the desk drawer, and asked, "Please tell me everything you know about the Acme job."

"I know the man who engineered it," declared Merlin. "He's involved in lots of other crimes, too. And he's right here in Midvale."

"Right under our noses, eh?" Lieutenant Hutchins drew a heart on the pad and pierced it with an arrow. *Another crank,* he thought.

"Was there a big diamond robbery here lately?" said Merlin.

Hutchins and Caddy exchanged glances. "Maybe he means that diamond merchant who was slugged last August," Caddy suggested.

"Did you ever find out who did it?" asked Merlin.

"No," Hutchins admitted.

"Have the diamonds ever turned up?"

Hutchins shook his head.

"The same man is responsible for that crime," said Merlin.

Hutchins stood up and stretched. "Okay," he said. "Where do we find this one-man crime wave?"

"In the courthouse!"

Hutchins sat down abruptly. He looked at Caddy. Caddy looked at him. They both looked at Merlin.

"Who is it?" said Hutchins cautiously.

"Judge Holmsby!"

The lieutenant threw his pencil down on the desk. "That's not very funny!" he shouted.

"I'm telling you the truth." Merlin rubbed his damp palms along his trouser legs. "Judge Holmsby is responsible for the payroll robbery, the theft of the diamonds, and for other crimes I don't have details on."

Hutchins walked to the window and stood looking down into the street. "I don't suppose you have any evidence to support this wild charge," he said at last.

"I overheard him mentioning his crimes," said Merlin.

"That's not good enough," Hutchins told him. *But I sure wouldn't mind having something on that old stiffneck,* he said to himself.

"You investigate him, and you'll have plenty on the old stiffneck!" Merlin promised.

Hutchins jumped guiltily.

"We can't investigate him," declared Caddy. "He's giving the police a hard time right now. What'll he do if he finds out we're investigating him?"

"Caddy, that'll do." Hutchins waved him to silence. "We could, of course, investigate the other man and see what turns up."

"What other man?" asked Merlin.

"The one you heard him talking to," said Hutchins.

"But—but there was no other man."

Hutchins was confused. "You said you overheard him talking about his crimes. Who was he talking to?"

Merlin swallowed hard. He hadn't foreseen this complication. "Well, he wasn't really talking to anyone. He was sort of—sort of thinking."

"Out loud?"

"No, sir. To himself."

Caddy grinned. "It might be just a coincidence," he told Lieutenant Hutchins, "but Judge Holmsby suspended Mr. Jones's license for ten days."

"Is that so?" Hutchins nodded wisely.

"Yes, he did," Merlin explained, "but it wasn't fair because—"

"You're supposed to appear before him again next week," Caddy reminded Merlin.

"Yes, sir."

Hutchins seized Merlin by the arm and lifted him out of the chair. "You picked the wrong way to win friends and influence judges." He spoke through clenched teeth. "You not only could've gotten yourself in big trouble—you could've had us all in a mess."

"I'm not making things up to get even with the

judge," Merlin cried. "I'm telling you the truth!"

"Get out before we book you!" shouted Hutchins.

"You've got the wrong idea. I'm—"

"Out!" yelled Hutchins. "And never come back!"

9 A MADDENING DRIP

The next morning, Jennifer picked Merlin up at Mrs. Schmidt's. He looked pale and wretched, and as she drove the blue convertible to the college he said not a single word. Jennifer brooded about this through her nine and ten o'clock classes. Two hours of brooding time was about all that Jen would allow herself. At eleven she decided on action—or at least on a little heart-to-heart talk with her gloomy friend. She went to the women's lounge, repaired her lipstick, and combed her hair. Then she marched across the campus, out the gates, and over to the Campus Cafe.

Merlin was morosely polishing glasses at a serving table in the back of the cafe. Otherwise the restaurant was empty.

"Hi!" Jen waved cheerily and took her usual place at the corner table. Merlin put down his towel and went to fill two coffee cups from the urn. He set one cup in front of Jennifer and began sipping the other himself.

Jennifer got right to the point. "Merlin, you're not still worrying about that suspended license, are you?"

"No."

"Are you worried about Stanley?"

"A little, maybe." Merlin made damp circles on the table with the bottom of his cup. "I've really gone on to bigger things," he said.

"Bigger worries?"

Merlin nodded. "Stolen diamonds!" He leaned closer to Jen. "Maybe even a murder," he confided.

"Merlin!"

"I'm on the track of a big criminal." Merlin's voice was weary. "But no one will believe me."

Jen hesitated. She was not sure that even she believed Merlin. "How did you get on this criminal's track?" she asked at last.

"It's a secret. I can't tell anyone."

"Not even me?" Unconsciously, Jennifer had adopted the manner of a kindly nurse toward a recalcitrant patient.

"Especially not you," said Merlin.

"Well!" Jennifer dropped her sickroom manner. "If that's the way you feel about me, Merlin Jones. . . ."

Angrily, she picked up her purse.

"I'm not supposed to tell anyone," Merlin tried to explain. "But—but I *have* to, or I'll explode. Jennie, if I tell you, will you keep my secret?"

Jennifer put down her purse.

"Promise?" pleaded Merlin.

"I promise."

Merlin looked around. The restaurant was still empty. He edged closer to Jen and whispered, "I can hear people's thoughts."

"Oh, Merlin!" Jennifer throttled an impulse to laugh out loud. "No one can hear another person's thoughts."

Merlin was silent.

"And it's a good thing, too," Jennifer continued. "How terrible it would be if a girl's own thoughts weren't private."

"I had an accident in the lab the other night," Merlin said. "In some peculiar way, my brain was electrified and I can hear people's thoughts."

"You're just teasing!"

"Try me."

Jennifer shut her eyes. *Take my hand,* she thought.

Merlin put his hand over hers.

Astonished, Jen opened her eyes. She stared hard at Merlin, then thought, *Pick up the sugar bowl!*

Merlin let go of her hand and picked up the sugar bowl.

"Merlin, that's fantastic!"

"You believe me now?" said Merlin.

"I believe you. I don't like the idea of anyone eavesdropping on my thoughts, but I believe you. Is that how you got on the track of the big criminal?"

Merlin nodded.

"Who is he?"

Merlin glanced at the door. "Judge Holmsby," he said softly.

"Judge Holmsby!"

"Shhh!" warned Merlin.

Jennifer dropped her voice. "You must be mistaken."

"I'm not mistaken. I heard him thinking about crimes he's been involved in, and about a murder he's planning to commit."

"Murder! Merlin, are you sure?"

"Positive."

"Then there's only one thing to do. You have to turn

your information over to the police."

"Ha!" said Merlin. "I tried that. They don't believe me, and they're too scared of the judge to investigate."

"What will you do?"

"I'll have to conduct my own investi—"

"Shh!" Jen pointed toward the door. "Here he is."

Merlin looked around. "He's early. I'm surprised he'd come back here, after I dropped coffee on him yesterday."

The judge was hanging up his hat and overcoat. He took a slip of paper from his coat pocket, read it, then tucked it into the pocket of his suit.

"Can you hear anything?" Jennifer whispered. "Do you know what he's thinking?"

"That piece of paper was a reminder to him," Merlin said. "Don't forget to call the plumber to fix the leak."

"That's no help," said Jen.

"Maybe, maybe not." Merlin scratched his chin. "Say, Jennie, are you free at one thirty?"

"Yes. Why?"

"Meet me in front of the administration building right after lunch. I have to borrow some stuff from the custodian."

Worried but game, Jennifer appeared in front of the administration building promptly at one thirty. Merlin was nowhere to be seen, so she sat down on a bench near the entrance and prepared to wait.

"Psst!"

Jennifer looked around.

"Psst! Jennie! Over here!" Merlin beckoned from the basement entrance under the front stairway.

"Merlin, what's this all about?"

"Come down and see."

In a dusty basement room, Merlin proudly displayed his prizes: two worn but clean suits of coveralls, two strange caps made of soft cloth, and an enormous kit filled with huge wrenches. "The custodian said we could have this stuff as long as we bring it back by five," he said.

"Keen!" Jen fingered one of the caps. "What are we going to do with it? Haunt houses?"

"We're plumbers, and we're going to fix the leak at Judge Holmsby's." Merlin sat down on a crate and began to pull one of the suits of coveralls on over his clothes.

"But I can't plumb!" cried Jennifer.

"You don't have to. You can be the helper and carry the tools."

"You mean you want me to put this thing on?" Jennifer wrinkled her nose at the remaining coveralls.

"It's clean," said Merlin.

"I'll wreck my skirt," grumbled Jen, but she began to climb into the garment.

The coveralls were big enough for four girls the size of Jen. Merlin helped her roll up the pants legs and the sleeves. She put on a cap and tucked her long dark hair up under it. "How do I look?" she asked.

Merlin surveyed her with some amusement. "Not much like a plumber," he admitted. "Maybe if you took off the lipstick?"

"Of course. I forgot." She dug in her purse for a tissue.

"Now let me do the talking," cautioned Merlin.

"Okay," said Jen.

He picked up the tool kit and opened the basement door. "The coast's clear," he announced. "Where'd you park the car?"

"Right across the street," said Jennifer. "And don't worry. If anyone sees us they'll think we're being initiated into something—United Goons of Midvale, maybe," she said sarcastically.

Merlin and Jennifer got to the car unseen. Jen slipped behind the wheel.

"Judge Holmsby lives on Greenacre Road," Merlin told her, "near the golf course. I looked him up in the book."

Jennifer turned the key and put the car into gear. "Are you sure plumbers drive around in convertibles?" she asked.

Merlin shrugged. "Why not?"

"Maybe we ought to put the top up. It wouldn't look so sporty."

"So we're sporty plumbers. Let's go. We may not have much time."

Crouching low behind the wheel in the hope that she wouldn't be seen, Jennifer headed across town and out Greenacre Road. Several people stared as the blue convertible went by, and one small boy hooted, but otherwise the drive was without incident. It was just two o'clock when they pulled up in front of Judge Holmsby's house. It was a big late-Victorian structure, amply girdled with porches and trimmed with gingerbread frills. Like the judge, it had an air of aloof superiority. Even the lace curtains at the windows seemed starchier than any curtains had a right to be.

"You carry the tools," Merlin commanded. He handed the kit to Jennifer. She bent almost double under the weight.

"Merlin!" she protested.

"You have to carry the tools," he said. "You're the helper." He strode up to the front door, letting Jennifer stagger after as best she could.

"Don't you think you're carrying authenticity a bit far?" She heaved the kit up onto the porch.

"Quiet!" said Merlin. He rang the bell.

The door was opened so quickly that Merlin knew they had been watched from behind those lace curtains. "Judge Holsmby said there was a leak had to be fixed," he told the aproned woman who stood with one hand on the knob.

"You're the plumber?" She seemed suspicious.

"Yes, ma'am," said Merlin.

"What's that?" She pointed at Jen, wilting in her coveralls.

"That's my assistant."

"Good night!" said the woman. "Well, come on in.

In my day plumbers looked like plumbers. You two look like—like—" She stopped in the middle of the hallway and tried to think of a word to describe Merlin and Jen. Then, deciding that this was an impossible challenge, she waved them on. "I shouldn't complain," she confided. "It's a miracle the judge remembered to call *any* plumber. Keeping house for him is no easy job. If it was one of his roses ailing, you could be sure he'd have it attended to in a minute. It's in here."

She led the way into a book-lined room at the back of the house. "The faucet in the bathroom off this study has been drip-dripping like the Chinese water-torture for two months." She opened a door on the far side of the room. Merlin looked with professional interest at a faucet that was, indeed, drip-dripping steadily into the sink. A rusty stain marred the side of the otherwise spotless basin.

"The judge has been saying every night that tomorrow he'll call the plumber," complained the housekeeper.

Merlin turned the water faucets on and off in an efficient manner. "I think I know what the trouble is," he said. "We'll get right to it."

"Good. That drip-dripping was maddening." The woman plodded away through the study.

"Search the desk," said Merlin, the moment the study door had closed on the housekeeper.

Jennifer pulled out a desk drawer. She saw neat rows of pencils, several small pads of paper, a box of stationery, and a checkbook. "What am I supposed to be looking for?" she asked.

"Evidence. Currency that can be traced to the payroll robbery, diamonds, things like that."

Jennifer opened a second drawer. There were envelopes containing bank statements, canceled checks, and telephone bills long since paid. There were the stubs of two tickets to the Imperial Theater. There was an invitation to speak at a meeting of the Bay City Bar Association.

Jennifer shut the drawer. "Nothing!" she announced.

Merlin was systematically taking books from the shelves which lined the room. "Nothing here, either," he said. "No wall safe. Nothing hidden behind the books." He riffled through the pages of a heavy law book. "Nothing hidden in the books, either."

"Merlin, I'm scared. We can't be here too long."

"Okay." As systematically as he had taken the books down, Merlin began to replace them. "We'll put everything back and. . . . Hey, wait a minute!"

"What is it?" Jen asked.

"I found something. Look at these books!"

Merlin held out a bulky volume. Unlike most of the quietly bound tomes in the judge's library, this one was brightly jacketed. Jennifer read the scarlet lettering splashed across a white background: "*The Payroll Robbery* by Lex Fortis!"

"And *The Bank Swindle* by Lex Fortis," added Merlin, pointing to a second book, one with a bright green jacket. "And here's *The Forgery* by Lex Fortis. And there are more. You know what this means?"

Jen laughed. "It just means he likes the Lex Fortis mystery novels," she said. "I do, too."

"But there's a difference," insisted Merlin.

"Oh? What?"

"You just read them for amusement. Judge Holmsby keeps them in a place of honor in his library. Jen, this is where the judge gets his ideas for his crimes!"

"It is?" said Jen.

"From now on, I'm relentless," vowed Merlin. "I

won't leave a private thought in Judge Holmsby's head."

"Fine," Jennifer agreed. "But I think we should go now."

"Okay. Just a minute and I'll be through." Merlin headed for the bathroom.

"Merlin, what are you doing?"

"I'm going to fix this faucet," Merlin told her. "That drip-dripping can be maddening."

For two days Judge Holmsby stayed away from the Campus Cafe. Merlin served for those two days with one eye fixed on the door. He was absentminded and clumsy. He mixed up his orders. Once he poured hot coffee into a water glass; the tumbler promptly shattered.

"What if he never comes here again?" said Jen, on the third day. She was keeping her vigil at the corner table.

"He'll show up sooner or later," said Merlin. "He's bound to. There are only three restaurants in town."

"Maybe he's going home for lunch."

Merlin considered this a horrible possibility. If Judge Holmsby took to having all his meals at home, how would Merlin ever again eavesdrop on his thoughts?

But at one o'clock Merlin's worries evaporated. The judge came in, hung up his hat and coat, and sat down at a table near the wall. Merlin leaped to serve him.

"Mr. Jones." The judge nodded.

"Yes, sir." Merlin half filled a water glass for the judge.

"I hope you'll be careful with the coffee today," said Holmsby.

"I will, sir. I'm sorry about that; it was an accident."

"I hope so." Judge Holmsby waved aside the menu. "I'll have the salad," he said. "French dressing."

"Yes, sir." Merlin almost ran to the kitchen. He was back in moments with the salad, which he served neatly. Holmsby began to eat, and Merlin took up his post close behind his chair.

The results were disappointing, at first. Holmsby's thoughts centered on household bills and car repairs, the fact that his housekeeper, Mrs. Gossett, was suffering from a touch of lumbago, and a mild curiosity about whether or not the said Mrs. Gossett had remembered to give his blue suit to the cleaners.

Merlin intercepted a suspicious glance from Effie. He dived for the water pitcher and poured an inch of water into the judge's glass.

Gloria Mundi was looking pretty good this morning, thought the judge.

Merlin stepped away from the table, but not far away.

Very rewarding, reflected Holmsby. *Shows what good care will do.*

Merlin wondered who Gloria Mundi might be. He got a cup and saucer and the coffeepot, and stood beside the judge's table to pour.

Speaking of care, the judge told himself sternly, *I'd better find a way to take care of those diamonds.*

Merlin's hand shook as he put the coffee cup in front of the judge. He withdrew to the serving table and was back immediately with the water pitcher.

"That's the third time you've given me water," Judge Holmsby observed. Merlin jumped and let the glass overflow.

"Just trying to be helpful, sir," said Merlin.

"Well, spread it around a little," pleaded the judge. "Be helpful to someone else."

Merlin faded back out of Holmsby's line of vision.

Perhaps I could use Gloria Mundi for the job, thought the judge.

Merlin made a beeline for Jennifer's table. "We may have a lead!" he told Jen. "Look through the telephone directory; see if you can find a woman named Gloria Mundi."

Jen reached into her purse for pad and pencil. "How do you spell it?" she asked.

"I don't know. Try every way you can think of, but find out where she lives. She may be an accomplice!"

Jennifer disappeared into the phone booth. Merlin hurried back to the judge's table. Holmsby saw him coming, frowned, and quickly gulped the last of his coffee.

"Well, sir, how about some dessert?" Merlin picked up Judge Holmsby's salad plate.

"No, thanks. I don't eat desserts."

"We have something special today," urged Merlin. "Homemade peach pie!"

"I said no," insisted Holmsby.

Defeated, Merlin started for the kitchen.

Wait a minute! The judge's mind snapped into high gear. Merlin did a quick about-face and was back at the table.

Peach pits! Holmsby said to himself.

"What, sir?" asked Merlin.

"I didn't say anything," snapped Holmsby. Then,

after a moment, he said, "Bring me a plate of peach pits."

"Peach pits?" Merlin was incredulous.

"That's right. A plate of peach pits."

"Yes, sir."

Puzzled, Merlin went to the kitchen. He ignored the amused stares of the cook and piled a small dish high with peach pits. Merlin returned to the dining room, put the dish in front of the judge, hesitated, then went to the serving table and brought back a cream pitcher and sugar bowl.

The judge was pleased with the unusual dessert, though he didn't put cream and sugar on it. Instead, he picked up a pit and examined it closely. *It's perfect!* he thought. *I split them in half, scoop out the insides, and place a diamond in each one. Then I glue the halves together and dig a hole under the rosebush. I'll try it this afternoon as soon as I get home, and see what I have to do to cover up traces of digging.*

Holmsby looked up and saw Merlin beside him. "Do you want something?" he asked.

"Oh, no, sir," said Merlin. "I, er, I just thought you might like the peach pits a la mode." It was a silly suggestion, but it was the best Merlin could do.

The judge was jovial. "No," he declared. "These are fine. They're just fine."

Having learned all he needed to know, Merlin left the judge to his peach pits and went to the phone booth.

"I found two Mundys," Jen told him. "There's a Maundy and three Mondays. But no Gloria."

"Never mind." Merlin was triumphant. "The whole case is busted wide open. Now the police will believe me!"

Merlin completed the formalities of lunchtime at the Campus Cafe. He added the judge's bill, noting courteously that there was no charge for the peach pits. He helped Effie clear off the tables and put out fresh place mats. Then he hung up his white coat, put on his sweater, and walked quietly down the street, through the town square, and up to the police station.

After a brief encounter with the desk sergeant, Merlin was again sent up to Lieutenant Hutchins' bleak little office. Hutchins listened patiently as, step by step, Merlin recounted the story of his investigation of the judge. The lieutenant was skeptical, but, after a few demonstrations, Merlin had him convinced.

Hutchins led Merlin down the hall to a larger but equally barren office which was the domain of a Captain Loomis. Loomis, smaller than Hutchins, tight of face and short of temper, listened with open disbelief as Merlin plunged into the saga of Judge Holmsby's double life.

Merlin hadn't gotten very far before Loomis interrupted. "This the kid you were telling me about?" he asked Hutchins.

"That's right," said the lieutenant.

"The one that says old Holmsby's the mastermind behind the Acme payroll job and the diamond heist?"

"The very same," declared Hutchins.

Loomis snorted. "Why are you wasting my time with him?" he demanded.

Merlin experienced a sinking feeling in the pit of his stomach. This man wasn't going to believe him.

Lieutenant Hutchins was reassuring. "Tell the captain what you told me," he instructed Merlin. "Tell him how you first found out about the judge."

"I heard his thoughts," said Merlin.

Loomis grimaced. "What is this?" he snapped. "April Fools' Day?"

"Go ahead, kid," said Hutchins.

"I was doing some experiments with a form of electro-encephalograph—"

"Never mind the scientific stuff," advised Hutchins. "Show the captain how it works."

Merlin grinned. "Think of something," he told Loomis.

Loomis's face mirrored his disgust. *This kid's lost his marbles,* he told himself.

"I haven't lost my marbles," Merlin said. "Everything I've told you is true. I can read thoughts."

Impressed, but still doubtful, Loomis turned to the lieutenant. "Does Kohner still have the bank-job suspect in the polygraph room?" he asked.

Hutchins nodded. "The lie detector! That's a great idea!" He turned to Merlin. "We think this hood's one of the men who held up the Midvale Bank and killed a guard," he explained. "But we don't have any real evidence and we don't know who his partner is. The lie detector isn't much help. It tells us when he's probably lying, but it doesn't tell us what the truth is."

Merlin nodded. "Maybe I can help," he offered.

Hutchins and Loomis led the way, back down the

hall, past Hutchins' office, to a large room where a thin, dark-faced man was being given a lie detector test. The suspect was very cool and calm, completely in possession of himself. He ignored the instruments strapped to his arms and his chest. These instruments, Merlin knew, were designed to detect the slightest changes in respiration, blood pressure, and heartbeat. Such changes, theoretically, would indicate that the man lied.

Kohner, the policeman who was interrogating the suspect, ignored the arrival of Merlin, Loomis, and Hutchins. "Were you in the Midvale Bank yesterday?" he asked the suspect.

"Nope." The man spoke without a trace of emotion.

Kohner mopped at his neck with his hankerchief. "Did you hold up the Midvale Bank?"

"Nope."

Hutchins signaled to Merlin to stand behind the suspect and to one side. Merlin took his place out of the man's line of vision. He could see without being seen.

"Did someone help you hold up the bank?" Kohner was dogged.

"I already told you I didn't do it," said the man.

"Just answer yes or no, please," instructed a technician. He did not look up from the polygraph, where a stylus etched black lines on a roll of paper.

The suspect sighed. "Okay," he agreed.

Merlin concentrated on the man. *This whole roomful of cops couldn't track down a tired jaywalker,* was the contemptuous thought that Merlin was receiving from the suspect.

"Did someone help you hold up the bank?" Kohner was repeating the question for the hundredth time.

"Nope." *They can't make that rap stick if they put glue on it.*

"You getting anything?" Captain Loomis whispered.

Merlin nodded.

I got 'em up a tree, gloated the criminal inwardly.

"What's he thinking?" Loomis asked.

"He's thinking he's got you up a tree," said Merlin.

Loomis groaned. "He's right."

"Did you use a thirty-eight caliber Smith and Wesson?" asked Kohner.

"Nope." *Come on, coppers, give up. You can't pin nothin' on me. I want to catch up with my buddy in*

Westhaven. I want to start livin' it up.

Merlin leaned close to Kohner. "Ask him if his partner is in Westhaven," he whispered.

Kohner looked startled, but Captain Loomis nodded his consent. "Is your partner in Westhaven?" Kohner asked the suspect.

The criminal started, then quickly regained control. *That was just a lucky guess,* he told himself.

"Answer the question," Loomis insisted. "Is your accomplice in Westhaven?"

"No!"

The stylus on the polygraph vibrated.

They don't know nothin' about Lipton, the holdup artist comforted himself. *The rod is safe at the bottom of the river.*

Merlin whispered to Loomis. Loomis smiled, stepped forward, and pointed to the polygraph equipment. "We won't need this anymore," he told Kohner. "His partner confessed."

The thug gave a short, mirthless laugh. "That's the oldest trick in the book," he said.

"The Westhaven police picked up a man named Lipton," Loomis told him.

Merlin watched the man's face take on a dirty gray pallor.

"Lipton said you were the one who shot the bank guard." Captain Loomis was beginning to enjoy himself. "He said you threw the gun into the river."

"He's lyin'!" The man was out of the chair, tearing at the instruments fastened to his arms. "Lipton's a dirty rat!" he shouted. "The whole caper was his idea. The rod was his, too, and he's the one who drilled the guard. He ain't gonna pin that on me!"

"Take it easy," advised Captain Loomis. "Make yourself comfortable. Dictate your confession slowly." He turned to Kohner. "You can forget the polygraph," he told him. "We have something better." And he put his arm around Merlin's shoulder.

Exultant, Merlin trailed Loomis and Hutchins back to Loomis's office. "I never saw anything like that in thirty years of police work," said Loomis. He threw himself into the chair behind the desk. "We could have worked on him forever without getting anywhere at all."

Hutchins patted Merlin on the back. "You sure did the trick," he exclaimed.

"Thanks." Merlin was pleased, but he liked to keep his eyes on the ball. "Now to get back to the Holmsby case," he said. "The diamonds are hidden under a rose-bush in Judge Holmsby's backyard."

Loomis leaned forward. "How do you know?" he asked.

"I heard him plan to hide them. All we have to do is get a shovel and dig them up."

But Loomis still had doubts. "It's not really that simple," he told Merlin.

"Why not? If you don't have a shovel, I can get you one."

"Have you ever been in Judge Holmsby's backyard?" Loomis asked.

Merlin admitted that he hadn't.

"The judge is a rose fancier," Loomis explained. "He has hundreds of rosebushes."

Merlin was not dismayed. "We'll just dig till we find the right one," he said.

"We can't," Captain Loomis told him.

"Why can't we?"

"Before we can dig up the judge's yard," Loomis explained, "we'd have to get a search warrant."

"That's right," Lieutenant Hutchins put in.

"Okay, okay. Let's get a warrant. Who do we have to see for that?"

"Judge Holmsby!" chorused Loomis and Hutchins.

11

"If you're going out with Merlin, I don't see why you're wearing *that* thing." Mrs. Hartley, hovering in the doorway of Jennifer's room, watched her daughter pull on the ancient coveralls which Merlin had borrowed once more from the college custodian.

"We're going to do some gardening," Jen explained to her mother.

"At night?"

"It's a very special kind of gardening," said Jen. "We're looking for peach pits." She began to pin her hair on top of her head.

"But, Jennie, if you and Merlin want peach pits, I've a whole basket of peaches downstairs ready for canning."

Jen pulled the custodian's soft cloth cap down over her forehead and turned sideways in front of the mirror to examine the effect. It was pretty awful. "They're very special peach pits," she told her mother.

"All right, Jennie. But you do look odd. Will you be warm enough?"

"Sure, Mom."

"Don't be too late," warned Mrs. Hartley.

"I won't." Jen kissed her mother on the forehead.

As she went down the stairs Jen heard her father call from his bedroom. "Where's Jennie going?" he asked.

Mrs. Hartley answered from Jen's room. "She and Merlin are going to do some gardening."

"At night?" Jen heard her father's feet hit the floor with a thud, and she scurried for the front door.

"It's a very special kind of gardening, dear." Mrs. Hartley's voice floated down the stairs. "Would you like some nice sliced peaches before you go to bed?"

The door clicked shut behind Jennifer. Reflecting that her mother was quite a peach herself, Jen got into Merlin's car, started the motor, and backed out of the driveway.

The streets were almost deserted. Jennifer made the run to Mrs. Schmidt's house in less than ten minutes. Merlin was waiting in the shadows near the garage. He came forward as the convertible slid to the curb. Like

Jen, he wore coveralls. "Did you have any trouble at home?" he asked.

"No, but let's hurry and get this over with."

Merlin tossed two shovels into the back seat, then got into the car and closed the door gently.

"Mom couldn't understand why the coveralls," said Jen.

"We don't want to be recognized."

"I didn't think I'd tell her just that," Jen laughed. Gears meshed smoothly and the car began to move. "I still think the police should be doing this," said Jen.

"They can't," said Merlin. "Or at least they won't. They won't touch a shovel to Judge Holmsby's backyard without a search warrant."

Jen made an exasperated noise between her teeth. "It frosts me," she said. "He can get away with murder just because he's a judge and everyone's scared of him."

"It isn't murder yet," Merlin reminded her.

"Not so far as we know," was Jen's grim reply.

The car turned into Greenacre Road and approached the high-hipped Victorian house belonging to the Honorable Curtice C. Holmsby. Jennifer slowed almost to a crawl.

"The lights are on," Merlin observed. "He's still up. Cruise down the street a way and then turn around and park."

Jen did as she was told. The car came to a stop in the shadow of a huge elm tree.

"He should be turning in soon," Merlin said hopefully.

Jen glanced at her watch. "My mother said not to be late."

"We have plenty of time. Wait a minute. He's coming out!"

The front door of the house had opened. Merlin and Jen saw the judge emerge. He had a square, paper-wrapped parcel under his arm. The housekeeper, Mrs. Gossett, stood in the doorway. "I'm glad it's over with," Jen and Merlin heard her say. "You're always so crotchety when you're having trouble finishing up one of your crimes."

"Good night," breathed Merlin. "The housekeeper's in on it, too."

"No more, Mrs. Gossett," the judge said. "I am now genial Judge Holmsby, a man whose feelings would remain unruffled in the face of disaster."

"Oh, Merlin," whispered Jen, "do you think we're too late?"

"I don't see how," Merlin answered. "He only buried the diamonds this afternoon. They must still be there."

The judge went whistling down the street, turned the corner, and disappeared from view. On the first floor of the house, lights blinked out, one by one, until only a dim light in the front hallway burned. Then, in an upper room, a light flashed on.

"She's going to bed," Merlin concluded. "Now's our chance. Come on."

Quietly, Merlin and Jen got the shovels out of the back of the car and crept around to the wall which marked the west end of the Holmsby property. Merlin tossed the shovels, one at a time, over the wall into the backyard. Then he grabbed the top of the wall, pulled himself up, and turned to help Jen.

"Merlin, what's the charge for what we're doing?" Jen asked.

Merlin got a good grip on the back of her collar and her belt and heaved. "Trespassing, I suppose," he grunted. "That is, if the police catch us."

Jen floundered until she got a leg over the wall.

"I suppose it could be prowling, or malicious mischief," Merlin said thoughtfully. "I think they're just misdemeanors."

"That's a comfort."

Merlin dropped into the darkness of the Holmsby rose garden. After an instant of indecision, Jen jumped after him. She landed up to her ankles in soft loam.

"Maybe you should have told Captain Loomis what you were going to do," Jen whispered into the darkness.

"Are you nuts?" Merlin's voice was so close that Jen jumped. "He'd never have stood still for it. What's the matter, Jennie? Are you getting cold feet?"

"No. Not exactly." Jen kicked one tennis shoe, trying to dislodge some of the dirt.

"Then let's get busy." Merlin produced a flashlight and snapped it on. Its beam danced across the garden.

"Merlin!" Jennifer gasped. "There are *hundreds* of roses. Which one are the diamonds buried under?"

"I don't know." Merlin set the flashlight on an empty birdbath. It reflected dimly off the brick wall. "We'll just have to dig them up one at a time," he said. "You start over there and I'll begin here."

"All right. But I hate to do it." Jen picked up a

shovel. "They're so beautiful," she mourned.

Merlin didn't answer. He was busy digging.

The rosebushes by the west wall went first. As each one toppled, Merlin and Jen stooped to examine the earth under the roots. They found nothing. Doggedly, they tackled the roses that grew against the house. There, too, the search was unrewarded.

"It's getting late," Jen said at last. "The judge might be coming back any minute, and my mother will be worried."

"It won't be long now," Merlin predicted. "There are only a few bushes left. The diamonds just have to be under one of them."

Merlin's shovel grated at the base of a large, particularly handsome rosebush. He worked the roots loose, then dropped the shovel and lifted. The bush came free. Merlin tossed it aside and groped in the cavity left by the rosebush.

"I've got 'em!" he gasped.

"Are you sure?" Jen flew for the flashlight and focused it on Merlin's hand. There, encrusted with dirt, were three large peach pits.

"I've got 'em! I've got 'em!" Merlin repeated.

Jen snapped off the flashlight. "Let's get out of here," she pleaded.

Merlin started to his feet. But before he could make another move, he was transfixed, caught in the beam of a powerful searchlight.

"If you have weapons, drop them!" commanded a frightfully familiar voice. "Raise your hands above your head!"

Jennifer's heart seemed to leap up between her ears. She dropped her shovel and the flashlight and put her hands up. Merlin stood defiant, clutching his peach pits.

"We have you surrounded!" called the voice behind the light. "Come forward peacefully and no one will get hurt!"

Merlin stepped forward. "Hi, Caddy," he said softly.

Caddy remained invisible behind the light, but Lieutenant Hutchins strode into view. "Merlin Jones!" he exclaimed. "I should have known."

"What's going on out here?" Judge Holmsby suddenly loomed up behind the lieutenant.

"Prowlers, Judge!" Mrs. Gossett lumbered forth from the shelter of the darkened kitchen. "I heard 'em in the garden and I called the cops, and—" She stopped in her tracks. "Why, these aren't prowlers," she said. "These are those nice plumbers that fixed the leak in the bathroom." She sounded quite pleased with this discovery.

The judge wasn't concerned about the leak in his bathroom. He had caught sight of the devastation in his rose garden. "Gloria Mundi!" he cried, snatching up the rosebush that Merlin had just dropped.

"Gloria Mundi's not here now," Merlin told him. "She won't be able to help you. I've got the goods on you this time."

The judge mourned over his rosebush. "This is the only polyantha I have that has orange flowers," he said.

"Merlin!" A light dawned on Jen. "Gloria Mundi is a rose!"

Merlin ignored her. "Arrest that man!" he shouted, pointing at the judge. "Here are the stolen diamonds!" He waved his three peach pits proudly under Lieutenant Hutchins' nose.

"Those are diamonds?" Hutchins was unmoved. "I would've sworn they were peach pits."

"Of course they're peach pits. The diamonds are inside."

Judge Holmsby put the rosebush gently on the

ground and stared at Merlin. "I don't understand it," he said. "I don't understand it at all. But in some way, young man, you've found me out."

Lieutenant Hutchins was astounded. He knew that Merlin had strange powers, but he had hardly expected the judge to give in this easily.

"I suppose it's time for me to make a confession," said Holmsby. "Shall we go inside, and do this in a civilized fashion?"

He led the way. Hutchins was close behind, with Merlin and Jen trailing in his wake. Caddy Lightfoot brought up the rear, remembering to snap off his searchlight only after Mrs. Gossett glared at him inside the judge's study.

The judge sat on the edge of his desk, facing the others. "I suppose what I have to say will be something of a shock to you," he began.

"Maybe not as much of a shock as you think," said Hutchins.

The judge smiled. "Maybe not," he admitted. "It's been my experience that an alert police force is never fooled for very long."

Lieutenant Hutchins smirked, and Merlin had

a sudden strange urge to hit him with some heavy, blunt instrument.

"For many years now," said Judge Holmsby, "I've been living a double life. During the day I've been a judge, dedicated to upholding the law. At night I've lived a life steeped in crime."

Hutchins interrupted to warn the judge that anything he said might be used as evidence against him.

"Thank you," said Judge Holmsby. "But before I go into details, I would like to ask that you treat me with leniency and consideration."

"No deals," said Hutchins. "Not until I've heard your full confession."

They really enjoy having me over a barrel, thought the judge.

"Why shouldn't they, Judge Holmsby?" asked Merlin. "Don't you enjoy having other people over a barrel?"

Holmsby was startled.

"Yes," said Merlin. "I heard what you were thinking."

"You heard my thoughts?" Holmsby couldn't believe what he was hearing.

"That's how we got on to you, Judge," Hutchins explained. "This young fellow got himself electrified in some way so he can tune in on what you're thinking. As a forward-looking police force, naturally, we take advantage of the latest scientific developments."

Again Merlin had an almost overwhelming impulse to strike the lieutenant.

"That's very interesting," said Judge Holmsby. "But you don't have to read minds to learn about my crimes. You can find out by reading books." He pointed toward the shelves behind him. "As Lex Fortis, I write novels about crime," he told them. "I don't commit crimes— except in the opinion of certain literary critics."

The silence in the room was so profound that Merlin could hear his own heart beat.

"The thoughts young Mr. Jones overheard related to my latest book," the judge went on. "It has to do with a jewel robbery. I finished it this afternoon and mailed it to my publisher this evening."

Lieutenant Hutchins didn't seem to know what to do with his feet—or his hands—or his hat.

"I've been as good a judge as I know how," continued Holmsby. "Perhaps I've been too hard on the police.

I'm prepared to be a little more reasonable in the future, if. . . ."

"If what?" asked Hutchins.

"If the police agree to keep the fact that I am Lex Fortis a secret."

"It's a deal!" Hutchins was enormously relieved.

Caddy Lightfoot, unseen by either the judge or Hutchins reached over and took a peach pit from Merlin's hand. He pried the two halves open. "There's nothing in it!" he said.

"You were expecting diamonds, maybe?" said the unhappy Merlin.

Jen patted his arm. "It was an honest mistake, Merlin," she whispered. "It could have happened to anyone."

Judge Holmsby glimpsed Merlin's woebegone expression and waggled a stern finger. "This is what happens, Mr. Jones, when you go prying into other people's thoughts."

"I'm sorry, your Honor. I really am sorry. And I didn't mean to pry into anyone's thoughts. It was an accident."

"An accident? Was it an accident that you dug up

every rosebush in my garden?"

"No, sir. And I'll put them all back. But it was an accident that I heard you plotting to bury stolen diamonds under the rosebushes. You see, sir, I'd been working on a device—a machine to measure brain capacity. . . ."

The judge shuddered. "Have I seen this machine, Mr. Jones?"

"Oh, yes, sir. Of course. In court. Well, I short-circuited it, accidentally, in the lab, and my brain got sort of electrified, and now I can hear everything everyone's thinking. And it's all a big mess, when all I wanted to do in the first place was help Stanley!"

"Stanley?"

"The chimpanzee."

"Ah, yes. I remember Stanley. Well, your motives are admirable, Mr. Jones, but remember this: A man's home is his castle, but a man's mind is even more precious and more private. No one has the right to violate the privacy of another person's mind. Or, to put it more simply, Mr. Jones, stop butting into other people's thoughts!"

"I'll remember that, sir," said Merlin.

"And one more thing, young man. . . ."

"Yes, sir."

"I believe we are destined to meet again—in court?"

"Yes, your Honor," sighed Merlin. "Monday morning, at ten o'clock."

12   **THE GREAT EXPERIMENT**

Merlin's appearance before Judge Holmsby turned out to be not at all dreadful. After warning Merlin that a license to drive an automobile is not a right but a privilege which can be withdrawn if it is abused, the judge restored Merlin's license. Then he beckoned him to approach the bench.

"I'd like to talk to you in private," the judge told Merlin. "Could you drop by my home for a minute tonight?"

Merlin was in no mood to refuse the judge anything. He quickly agreed, and the judge dismissed him. Merlin lost no time in joining Jennifer in the corridor.

"I had a feeling he'd return your license," Jen said happily. "What did he say to you there at the end? I couldn't hear."

"He wants me to see him at his house tonight."

"What for?"

"I don't know." Merlin looked surprised. "You know,

Jen, I really *don't* know," he said. "I couldn't tell what he was thinking. As a matter of fact, I haven't heard any thoughts at all today. Maybe the charge is gone."

"Let's find out. What am I thinking?" Jen shut her eyes and concentrated.

Merlin took a wild guess. "You want a hot fudge sundae?"

"Wrong! I was thinking about your pet, Stanley. The charge must be gone. Oh, Merlin, I'm so glad!"

"Me, too. And speaking of Stanley, I wonder how he's doing."

"I don't know," said Jen. "It's been a little busy out lately to worry about chimpanzees."

Merlin, suddenly glum, led the way to the car. "Let's go to see him," he said.

"Stanley?"

"Yes, Stanley."

"Now, Merlin, you know you're not supposed to go near him. You'll get into trouble again if you do."

"Okay." Merlin was agreeable. "You go to see Stanley and I'll wait outside for you. We can get him a present."

"No bananas," Jen reminded him. "You promised Norman. Remember?"

"Apples?" said Merlin.

Jennifer laughed. "Apples," she agreed.

But, half an hour later, Jen rejoined Merlin outside the science building and had to report that the apples were a failure.

"I put them right into his cage," she told Merlin, "but he wouldn't even look at them. And he hadn't touched his breakfast. It was still there in his dish."

"Was Norman there?"

"No. I think he's got a class this hour. Merlin, Stanley's sick."

"Or lonely," suggested Merlin. "Or maybe just plain scared."

"Of Norman?"

"Who else? I'm going to talk to Professor Shattuck today. Maybe he can do something about it. He ought to; Stanley really belongs to his department."

But when Merlin went to Shattuck's office, he found a note pinned to the door. Shattuck was in Cedar Crest for the day.

"I'll talk to the professor tomorrow," Merlin told Jen as he drove her into town that evening. "He's a good guy; he'll do something about Stanley."

"Like what?" Jen demanded.

"I don't know," Merlin admitted. "Maybe Stanley could stay with me for a while."

"Mrs. Schmidt would just love that," Jennifer giggled.

"She wouldn't mind. Really, she wouldn't. She likes animals, except for one or two dogs I know. As long as Stanley got along okay with Mittens. . . ."

"The cat?"

Merlin nodded. "Feistiest cat on the block," he said, "courtesy of the Merlin Jones Self-Improvement Association. And would you mind, Miss Hartley, waiting in the car while I go and find out what Judge Holmsby wants? Or do you want to come in with me?"

"No, I don't want to come in with you. Besides, didn't Judge Holmsby say it was private?"

"Yes, he did at that." Merlin turned into Greenacre Road and slowed to a sedate twenty miles an hour.

"I don't think the judge will pop out of the bushes and give you a ticket right here," said the amused Jen.

"You never know. Just the thought of Judge Holmsby tends to inhibit me." Merlin rounded a bend in the road and came into sight of the judge's house.

"Now don't keep me waiting all night," said Jennifer.

Merlin parked. "The judge said it would only be a minute," he reminded her.

Judge Holmsby answered the door himself. Mrs. Gossett, the outspoken housekeeper, was not in evidence. For some reason this made Merlin feel more comfortable.

The judge got right to the point as soon as he and Merlin were seated in his study. "Mr. Jones," said the judge. Then he stopped and started over. "Merlin, I wanted to talk to you about your experiments."

Merlin felt this was very slippery ground. "My experiments?" he asked.

"Yes. Particularly your experiments in hypnotism. Some time ago, you told me you had hypnotized that chimpanzee . . . what's his name?"

"Stanley," supplied Merlin.

"Yes, Stanley. And a cat?"

"Mittens," Merlin said. "My landlady's cat."

"Yes. You were, if I remember correctly, trying to bring about changes in the personalities of these animals."

"That's right."

"Have you done much work with hypnosis?" the judge asked.

"No, sir," said Merlin. "I've only worked with Stanley and with Mittens. I did help Mittens, and I felt that I could help the chimpanzee, too."

"And perhaps you can help me," suggested Judge Holmsby.

Merlin did not like the direction the conversation was taking, so he didn't help it along. He held his tongue.

"What I want," said the judge, "is information about hypnosis. As you know, I finished a book recently. I want to start a new Lex Fortis mystery, and I think that hypnotism might be useful."

"Well, I'll give you whatever information I can, Judge Holmsby," said Merlin, "but there are men in the psychology department at the college who know a lot more about it than I do."

"But you're one of the few in Midvale who know that I write crime novels," Holmsby pointed out. "If it got out that I was Lex Fortis, I'd have no privacy left. I can't ask the kind of questions I need to without people becoming curious."

"That's true," Merlin agreed. "All right. I'll help if I can."

"Good! I don't want to take up much of your time tonight. I'm just blocking out an idea—a plot about a highly respected member of a community who commits crimes while under the influence of hypnotism."

"Well, Judge, I—"

"Wait a minute," cautioned the judge. "The man who's committing the crimes isn't actually responsible. In fact, he doesn't even know of his own guilt. The interesting angle is that he joins in a hunt to find the criminal, not knowing that he's searching for himself!" The judge sat back in his chair, a cocksure smile on his face. "How do you like it?" he demanded.

"It's very interesting," murmured Merlin.

The judge took this for unqualified praise. He glowed. "I thought you'd appreciate it," he told Merlin. "Now I want everything to be absolutely realistic."

"Then it's no good," said Merlin.

The judge was indignant. "What do you mean, it's no good? What makes you a literary critic?"

"I'm not," Merlin said.

"Then why are you throwing out the plot of my new

novel?" the judge demanded angrily.

"Oh, it's a great plot. But it isn't realistic."

"And why not?"

"Because," explained Merlin, "most authorities agree that an honest man can't be hypnotized into committing a crime."

"Oh!" The judge was completely deflated, but only for a moment. "What if the hypnotist ordered him to?" he asked brightly.

Merlin shook his head. "A person in hypnosis will not do anything that violates his moral code."

It was a staggering blow. The judge got up and paced back and forth in front of the fireplace.

"I'm sorry, Judge Holmsby," said Merlin.

"Shhh! I'm thinking."

The pacing continued. The judge rubbed his face and wrinkled his brow. At last he stopped near the hearthrug. "You said *most* authorities agree. . . ."

"That's right," Merlin confirmed.

"That means there are some who believe that an honest man *could* be hypnotized into committing a crime."

"I think maybe *some* do," Merlin said. "I could research it for you, Judge, and give you a concensus."

"No. I've got a better idea. We'll test it ourselves." He threw himself into his chair. "You hypnotize me," he ordered. "Try to get me to commit a crime. Pick something small. Nothing felonious, of course. A tiny misdemeanor will do."

Merlin was reluctant. "Hypnotizing a human is a big responsibility," he pointed out. "I'm not sure I'm ready for it."

"Nonsense!" said the judge. "I'll take full responsibility."

"Well, all right."

"Good. What do I do?"

"Just relax," said Merlin. "Look at that lamp. Keep staring at it and relax."

The judge obeyed.

"Let your muscles go slack," Merlin told him. "Concentrate all your thoughts on my voice and on nothing else."

Merlin's voice became a low, monotonous sing-song. "You feel heavy . . . heavy . . . heavy. Sleep is washing over you. It is hard to keep your eyes open. You're sleepy, very, very sleepy. Your eyes close."

The judge quietly closed his eyes.

"You are now in a hypnotic trance," Merlin said. "You cannot open your eyes no matter how hard you try. Try, Judge Holmsby. Try to open your eyes."

The judge strained, trying to lift his lids. His eyes remained closed.

"Now you can open your eyes," said Merlin.

The judge opened them and stared dully at Merlin.

"Extend your right arm," Merlin instructed.

Again the judge obeyed.

"Your arm is now as rigid as a steel bar," Merlin said. He took Holmsby's arm between his two hands and pressed down as hard as he could. The arm remained stiffly outstretched.

"Good!" said Merlin. "Now for a crime."

This wasn't so easy. It had to be a small crime, not a felony. Merlin realized that swiping garbage cans or dismantling people's front gates might do, but these things lacked style. Even a misdemeanor should show some imagination. After a few minutes' thought, Merlin had it. It was the perfect little white crime!

"Judge Holmsby," Merlin said, "at exactly nine o'clock tonight you will leave this house carrying a large bag. You will go to the Midvale campus, enter the psychology lab, and steal the chimpanzee from its cage."

Merlin smiled inwardly at the thought of the distinguished Judge Holmsby making off with a chimpanzee. "Bring the chimp home," he ordered the judge. "Put it to bed, and then go to sleep yourself. You will awaken from your sleep at the usual time tomorrow morning, and you will feel relaxed and refreshed."

The judge said nothing.

"Do you understand what you're to do?" asked Merlin.

"Yes," said the judge.

"Good. Well, good night, Judge Holmsby."

"Good night," replied the judge.

Merlin was almost out the door before he remembered that Judge Holmsby's arm was still stiffly outstretched. "You can lower your arm now," Merlin told him.

The judge did so, and Merlin went out to his car.

"What took you so long?" Jen asked.

"I hypnotized the judge," Merlin told her.

"What on earth for?"

Merlin chuckled. "To get him to steal the chimp from the psych lab."

"Merlin, you didn't!" Jen was paralyzed with shock.

"I did. I told him to leave his house at nine sharp with a big bag and go to the lab to get the chimp."

"How could you? A thing like that is sure to end up with you in trouble!"

Merlin laughed and started the motor. "There's nothing to worry about," he assured her. "First of all, the judge asked me to do it. He wants to test the theory that a man can't be hypnotized into doing something that's contrary to his moral code."

"But suppose the theory's wrong?" Jennifer reached over and turned off the ignition.

"Most authorities agree that it's right, so nothing will happen. Look! It's nine o'clock now, so the authorities are proven right."

"No, they're not." Jennifer pointed at the judge's house.

Judge Holmsby appeared on his front porch. His topcoat collar was turned up around his face and his hat was pulled down over his eyes.

"He's got a laundry bag under his arm!" said Jen. "You see. Those authorities are wrong. The judge is going to steal the chimp!"

"Not necessarily." Merlin was still unconcerned.

"What else would he be doing with a laundry bag?"

"Going to pick up his laundry?"

"At this hour of the night?" said Jen. "Don't be silly. And why is he sneaking around that way?"

Merlin had to admit that the judge certainly was sneaking around. He headed for the garage on tiptoe, being careful to keep in the shadow of the house.

"Maybe we'd better follow him," Merlin conceded. He started the engine and, when the judge's black sedan backed out of the drive, he began to tail it, keeping a careful half-block between himself and Holmsby.

"He's heading straight for the campus," Jen observed.

"Yes," said Merlin. "He seems to be trying to obey the hypnotic command."

They were passing through the open gates of the college. "Trying!" exclaimed Jen. "He's succeeding."

"Not on your life," Merlin declared. "At the last moment his basic honesty will assert itself. He won't go through with it."

The judge's car pulled up in front of the science building. "His basic honesty had better hurry up," worried Jennifer.

Merlin cut his lights and glided into the parking lot. He watched the judge get out of his car and disappear into the shadows near the entrance to the building.

"Merlin, he's going to do it," whispered Jen. "You've got to stop him."

Merlin got out of the car and ran toward the building. He saw the judge silhouetted briefly in the doorway, but when he reached the first floor hall it was deserted. Merlin made straight for the psych lab.

The lab was lighted only by a single small bulb in the ceiling. Merlin stopped halfway down the stairway. A subdued scrabbling came from the cages which housed the white rats. "Judge Holmsby, are you there?" Merlin called.

No one answered, and Merlin came on down the stairs. Stanley's cage was in deep shadow beyond the desk. "Stanley!" said Merlin. "Stanley. Hey, boy! You there?"

There was no sound from the chimpanzee. Merlin felt his way around the desk. The cage door stood open. Stanley was gone!

Behind Merlin, something moved. Merlin whirled and saw Judge Holmsby. He was still bundled to the ears, and he looked oddly stooped and misshapen in the dim light. He darted toward the stairs, and Merlin leaped, gaining the bottom of the stairway ahead of the judge.

"Judge, we have to return him or there'll be trouble." Merlin kept his tone as even as possible.

"Return who?" The judge was all astonished innocence.

"You know who I mean," said Merlin. "The chimpanzee."

"Chimpanzee?" The judge's smile dripped with criminal cunning. "I don't know anything about any chimpanzee," he said.

The judge's topcoat billowed out in front, and a hairy black hand crept up from under it to clutch at the judge's necktie.

"I mean the chimpanzee you're hiding under your coat." Merlin's tone was stern. "I see him, and—"

Merlin never finished the sentence. Holmsby, trapped, let go with a roundhouse right that caught Merlin square on the jaw. Red lights flashed before Merlin's eyes. He fell, jarring himself on outstretched hands, then feeling concrete cold and smooth against

his face. He was dimly aware of someone stepping over him, of footsteps on the stairs, and of a door slamming.

"Merlin! Speak to me!"

Merlin raised himself on one elbow and blinked. He was on the floor of the lab. Jennifer knelt next to him, her face grave and worried.

"I'm—I'm all right," Merlin told her. He felt his jaw and winced.

"He got away," cried Jen. "He took Stanley and got away in his car. I saw him. He's like a desperate criminal!"

With Jen's help, Merlin got painfully to his feet. "It's interesting that he has such a strong drive to obey the hypnotic command," he said.

"It's very interesting," said Jen. "It's also very dangerous."

"Not really," Merlin told her. "We can let him play out the rest of the command. He'll take the chimp home and go to sleep. Then I can slip in, get Stanley, and bring him back here."

"And I thought we were going to the movies," sighed Jen. "All right. Let's get it over with."

Jen fidgeted on the drive back to Greenacre Road,

but Merlin was serene and unruffled. He had forgotten his aching jaw; he was calmly turning over in his mind the possibility that the experts might be wrong—that an honest man might be hypnotized into committing a crime. It would be an interesting subject to explore with Professor Shattuck, Merlin decided.

Merlin parked under the elm tree near Judge Holmsby's house and quietly checked the garage. The black sedan was there, its hood still warm. Lights showed behind two long windows above the front porch of the house.

"We'll have to give him time to get to sleep," Merlin told Jen. Even as he spoke, the lights went out.

"There he goes," Jen murmured.

One of the windows went up noisily.

"I'm glad that he likes fresh air," said Merlin. "It makes it easier all around."

"How are we going to get in?" Jen asked.

"We are not going to get in," Merlin answered. "I am going to get in—up that trellis and over the roof of the porch. You are going to sit right here and wait for me."

Jen, who really had no taste for housebreaking, was

content with this answer. They waited without speaking for five minutes, then Merlin left the car and stole toward the house. Jen glanced around. The street was empty. She looked toward the house and saw Merlin go up the trellis quickly and easily. He crossed the porch roof in a half-stoop and disappeared into the open window. Jen waited, almost holding her breath. She could hear her wristwatch tick-tick excitedly in the stillness.

It seemed to Jennifer that Merlin had been gone for at least a week or two. Actually, it was only a minute or two before his head and shoulders thrust out through the open window. She saw him turn his head and put his finger to his lips. Beside him Stanley appeared, looking comically old and cautious. In docile imitation of Merlin, Stanley put his own long finger to his mouth.

Merlin took Stanley's hand and led the chimp across the roof to the trellis. Stanley balanced easily on the gutter and watched Merlin start down the trellis. Merlin got part of the way down, then beckoned to the chimp to follow. Stanley squeaked, hopped up and down a couple of times, grabbed the drainpipe at the corner of the roof, and came down swiftly, hand over hand.

Jen jumped out of the car and held the door open as Merlin hurried the chimpanzee toward her. "We have to get him back in his cage before he's missed," Merlin said. He lifted Stanley bodily into the back seat.

Jen jumped in and swung the door shut, and Merlin ran around the car to get behind the wheel. The need for stealth was over, and the motor roared as Merlin sped back toward the campus.

At the science building, Merlin coaxed Stanley, who was now quite sleepy, to uncurl himself and get out of the back seat. "Wait for me," Merlin told Jennifer. "I'll be right back."

"Don't get involved in an experiment or something and forget I'm here," warned Jen.

"I won't," Merlin promised. "I'll just put Stanley in his cage and come right out."

Stanley hopped along beside Merlin up the front steps and into the hallway of the building. At the doorway to the psych lab, Merlin stopped to listen. There was no sound. Even the hamsters and the rats were quiet. Satisfied, Merlin went down the stairway.

"Okay, hold it!" The voice cut through the darkness like a whiplash. Merlin jumped; Stanley squealed and clutched frantically at his hand.

A switch clicked, and every light in the lab flashed on. "I knew it!" Norman was triumphant. "I knew it had to be Merlin Jones!"

Caddy Lightfoot, flanked on one side by a very young, very thin policeman, and on the other side by the night watchman of the college, looked at Merlin over the sights of a regulation police revolver.

Norman swaggered away from the light switch. "I knew you wouldn't be able to leave that monkey alone!" he jeered.

"Chimp!" Merlin said.

Norman ignored the correction. "As soon as the watchman told me Stanley had been stolen, I knew who did it." Norman was enjoying himself tremendously.

"I was just putting him back," Merlin explained.

Norman took the cringing chimpanzee from Merlin and returned him to his cage. As the door swung shut on Stanley, Merlin saw the chimp put his arms up over his head. The gesture was revealing, and Merlin recalled Norman charging at Stanley with a yardstick.

"You beat him!" Merlin accused.

Norman didn't seem to hear this. "You shouldn't

have taken him," he gloated. "The judge warned you to stay away from here!"

"The judge will understand," Merlin said.

"He'll throw the book at you!" was Norman's gleeful prediction. He turned to Caddy and his cohort. "Arrest him!" he demanded.

Caddy took a firm grip on Merlin's arm.

"This is just an unfortunate little mixup," Merlin protested.

Norman laughed. "Now you'll both be where you belong," he told Merlin. "You and that monkey." He turned to rap on the top of Stanley's cage. "You'll both be behind bars!"

13

In the corridor of the courthouse the next morning, Merlin held a whispered conference with Jen. Caddy stood by, politely out of earshot but determined that Merlin would make no false moves.

"I feel so guilty," Jen lamented. "I was terribly angry with you last night. When I saw the lights go on in the lab, I didn't know you had fallen into the clutches of the law. I thought you'd started in on an experiment or something." Her eyes filled with tears. "I just got out of the car and walked all the way home," she said.

Merlin patted her arm. "I'm sorry, Jen," he told her. "I got things all bollixed up, as usual. And this time I'm in real trouble. Jen, the judge isn't going to remember that he was the one who stole the chimp."

Jen dabbed at her eyes and sniffed. "Why not?" she asked.

"Posthypnotic amnesia," said Merlin. "No one remembers the things they do under hypnosis."

"How awful!" exclaimed Jen. "You may be sentenced to years and years for something you didn't do."

"Don't get carried away," Merlin told her. "It isn't apt to be that bad. Besides, I have an idea. . . ."

"Merlin, don't!" Jen clutched at him. "Don't make a break for it. Escaped convicts are always caught."

"Will you please cut that out!" ordered Merlin. He was painfully aware of Caddy's amusement. "The problem is to make the judge remember that he stole Stanley last night."

"I'll just tell him!" Jennifer volunteered.

Merlin shook his head. "That won't do," he said. "We have to get past his conscious mind and through to his unconscious, where the memory of last night lies. I'll have to hypnotize him again."

"Merlin, you're crazy!" cried Jen. Caddy stared curiously and Jen blushed and lowered her voice. "How can you hypnotize him right in the courtroom?" she whispered.

"I'm going to try. There's an old oriental method of inducing hypnosis by gestures. And just in case it doesn't work—which it probably won't—would you see if you can find Professor Shattuck? Ask him to come here and to bring Stanley with him."

"Stanley? Why?"

Merlin summoned up a weak smile. "He might be my star witness," he told Jen.

Merlin's hearing before Judge Holmsby began with Norman Powell's testimony. Norman related, with lip-smacking relish, how he had received a telephone call from the night watchman at the college, and how the watchman had reported that a thief had entered the psych lab and taken one of the animals.

"When I found out which animal was missing," said Norman, "I knew right away who the thief was."

Judge Holmsby looked at Merlin, who immediately began to sway back and forth like an agitated fakir and wave his arms rhythmically in the air.

"I called the police," said Norman. "They arrived in a few minutes, and while we were there in the lab, the thief turned up."

Again the judge's gaze wandered to Merlin, and again Merlin swayed and waved his arms.

"We caught him red-handed," said Norman, "with the chimp—"

"Excuse me." The judge interrupted the testimony. "Mr. Jones," he said, "you can stop whatever it is you're doing. You can't plead insanity in a case like this."

Merlin gave up his attempts at long-range hypnosis.

"You can continue," Judge Holmsby told Norman. "Who was it you apprehended at the scene of the crime?"

Norman pointed. "It was Merlin Jones!"

The judge dismissed Norman then and called Merlin. "Did you steal that chimpanzee?" he asked.

"No, sir." Merlin's denial was firm.

"You had been warned to stay away from it," the judge reminded him.

"Yes, sir," agreed Merlin.

"Is it true, as Mr. Powell has testified, that you were found with the animal in your possession?"

Merlin admitted that it was.

"This certainly leads us to assume that you stole the animal for some experiments," said Judge Holmsby, "and that you were returning it when you were apprehended. Can you offer any other explanation?"

Merlin, of course, *could* offer another explanation. He considered doing just that, then decided that he could not possibly sit in Judge Holmsby's court and accuse the honored jurist to his face of chimp-napping. He shook his head. "No, sir," he said.

Judge Holmsby didn't like it. He didn't like it at all. Though Merlin appeared in his court with maddening regularity, the judge was beginning to develop a certain admiration for the boy. Merlin's offenses against the quiet and order of the community—if, indeed, they were offenses—were always prompted by a spirit of scientific inquiry, and not by malice. Judge Holmsby strongly suspected that there was some perfectly logical, though perhaps unusual, explanation for the theft of the chimpanzee.

"Is there anyone you want called to testify in your behalf?" the judge asked Merlin.

Merlin's eyes went to the back of the courtroom. Jen was there, and so was Professor Shattuck. Crouched in the seat next to Shattuck was Stanley.

"I do have a witness, your Honor," Merlin told the judge. "His name is Stanley."

Judge Holmsby had noted Merlin's apish friend in the back row. He put up his hand to hide a smile. *At least the boy is going to put up some kind of defense,* thought Holmsby, and, knowing Merlin Jones, it will be a pip.

"Call Stanley," Holmsby told the clerk.

"Stanley?" The clerk was surprised. Things were not usually this informal in Judge Holmsby's court. "Is Stanley his first name," he asked, "or his last name?"

"Both," said Merlin.

"Stanley Stanley!" cried the clerk.

Professor Shattuck stood up and led the chimpanzee toward the bench. The clerk, compelled by long habit, took a step toward the chimp and directed, "Raise your right hand, please." Ever docile, Stanley put up his hand.

"Are you out of your mind?" roared Judge Holmsby. "We do not swear in animals in this court!"

The clerk wilted like a tired daffodil and Professor Shattuck deposited his small charge in the witness stand and retired to the spectators' section of the courtroom.

Judge Holmsby addressed Merlin. "I want it understood, young man, that this is a court of law," he warned. "You are to behave seriously and with dignity."

"I will, your Honor," declared Merlin. "And I *am* serious about wanting Stanley to testify for me—though

I know he can't be sworn in as a witness. I want to use him to demonstrate the true relationship between this chimpanzee and Norman Powell."

"Very well," said Judge Holmsby. "You may proceed."

"Thank you, sir."

Merlin went to Stanley and held out his hand. The chimp took the hand and shook it happily.

"Come on, Stanley," said Merlin. "Come with me."

Stanley clutched Merlin's hand with both of his and swung himself down from the witness chair.

"This way, Stanley," coaxed Merlin. He led the chimpanzee toward the table where Norman sat. Stanley caught sight of Norman and hung back, pulling at Merlin's arm. He squealed and chattered softly.

"Now, Stanley," said Merlin. "No one's going to hurt you." He picked up the chimpanzee and carried him to Norman.

Norman edged away a little when Merlin put the chimp down on the table. Stanley looked around, saw Norman's face terribly near, shrieked, and leaped back into Merlin's arms. Merlin tried to push the chimp toward Norman, but Stanley cried piteously and wrapped his long arms around Merlin's neck.

With Stanley still clinging to him like a forlorn baby, Merlin returned to stand before Judge Holmsby. "Norman Powell has mistreated this animal," he accused. "I think I've proved that."

"I think you have, too," agreed the judge. He addressed Norman. "Mr. Powell, come here."

Glowering and scarlet, Norman obeyed.

"You should be ashamed of yourself," Judge Holmsby told him. "You have earned the fear of a helpless animal which was entrusted to your care. I intend to use whatever influence I have with the administration of Midvale College to see that you're relieved of responsibility for Stanley, and for any other animal. You may go, Mr. Powell."

Norman stood glaring like an affronted bull.

"I said you may go, Mr. Powell!" Judge Holmsby's voice was harsh. "Get out of my sight!"

Wordlessly, Norman went.

Judge Holmsby was surprised to note that his hands were trembling. He took out his handkerchief and wiped his palms, then dabbed at his brow. Merlin waited, holding Stanley by the hand. When he felt a little calmer, the judge went on.

"Mr. Jones," he said gently, "you have righted a wrong here today. Unfortunately, this has nothing to do with the matter before us. You have not offered any defense, and I have no alternative but to find you guilty as charged and to sentence you to sixty days."

"No!" cried Jen from the back of the courtroom.

"The sentence is suspended," said Judge Holmsby, "but for the duration of the sixty days, you will report to me once a week."

"No!" It was Jen again. She sped to the front of the room. "It's an injustice!"

Caddy jumped to catch her by the arm, but she dodged him neatly. "Merlin didn't steal the chimp!" she cried. "It was an experiment in hypnosis, and Merlin was just returning the chimp. Judge Holmsby was the one who stole it!"

"Mr. Jones," said Judge Holmsby, "your first reporting date is right now. Come to my chambers, and bring the young lady!"

At a signal from Judge Holmsby, Merlin took the leather-covered armchair in the judge's chambers. Stanley jumped up onto his lap, chattered happily and plucked at a loose thread in Merlin's sweater. Jen chose a straight chair and sat demurely, legs crossed at the ankles.

"Merlin, I want the truth," said Judge Holmsby. "Did I really steal the chimpanzee?"

"Yes, you did," Merlin told him.

"I witnessed it, your Honor," said Jen.

Stanley, gaining confidence, scrambled down from Merlin's lap and began an exploratory mission around the judge's desk. Holmsby patted him on the head, as one would pat a small child.

"What about the theory that honest men can't be hypnotized into committing crimes?" said Judge Holmsby.

It was a difficult question and Merlin took his time

about answering. "There are two possibilities," he said at last. "A theory is only a theory; it's not necessarily a fact. Either we've proved that the theory is false, or ... or. ..."

"Or what?" asked the judge.

"Or you're not an honest man," Jen said softly.

Judge Holmsby gave her a withering look.

"She doesn't mean that you're a thief," Merlin put in hastily.

"What does she mean then?" demanded Holmsby.

"Only that it's possible—that deep down within you, there may be. ..."

"You're trying to tell me that I have larceny in my heart," said the judge.

"I wouldn't put it quite that way, sir."

"However you put it," admitted the judge, "it may be quite true." He got up from behind his desk and began to pace back and forth between the bookcase and the door, his hands clasped behind him. "Perhaps the chief difference between me and some of the people I've sentenced is that I've been luckier than they," he said. "I've never been pressured by need or temptation." He stopped his pacing and brightened. "That will be the point of my new book," he announced. "We all have enough potential evil in us to make us a little more compassionate and a little more careful about passing judgment on our fellow man."

"And our fellow ape," suggested Merlin.

"Ape?" said Judge Holmsby.

Merlin nodded in the direction of the judge's desk. Stanley sat there, greatly enjoying one of the judge's cigars. Stanley wasn't smoking the cigar; he was eating it.

"That's enough of that, young fellow," laughed Holmsby. "You'll make yourself sick." Gingerly, he took the cigar from the chimp.

"I'm on the board of regents of the college," he told Merlin. "I think I can get permission for you to work with Stanley."

"I'd appreciate that, Judge," said Merlin.

"And, of course, this morning's conviction and sentence will be set aside."

"Thank you, your Honor."

Merlin persuaded Stanley to leave the judge's chair and come and sit beside him. The judge resumed his place behind the desk. "This means you won't have to

report to me once a week," he told Merlin, "unless, of course, you'd like to. I must admit, I'll be interested to know what new projects you undertake. You have a—er—you have a rather unusual turn of mind, Merlin Jones."

"Thank you, your Honor—I guess," laughed Merlin.

"And I'll put in a good word for you with Officer Lightfoot," offered the judge. "You seem to get arrested far too frequently."

"He certainly does," said Jen.

"I don't think you need to worry anymore about Caddy," Merlin told them. "We had a long talk last night, when I was . . . when I was in jail. You know, Caddy's quite a horticulturist. He's doing some interesting things with cross-pollination of fruit trees."

"You don't say!" Judge Holmsby was amazed.

"Yes," said Merlin. "I'm going to see if I can't help him. There's some good stuff in the college library on cross-pollinating. And he says I can use his garage if I want to continue my experiments with hydrocarbons."

"Oh, Merlin," groaned Jen. "No more green exhaust, please. My father will have a fit!"

"Well, now, wait a minute, Jennie," protested Merlin.

"I've gotten some very interesting results so far, and the possibilities are—"

Jen laughed. "I know," she said. "The possibilities are unlimited. I suppose I shouldn't complain. Hydrocarbons are bound to be a lot safer than hypnosis."

"Or mind reading," added the judge.

It was more than a week before Judge Holmsby saw Merlin Jones again, and then it was only a fleeting glimpse. Holmsby was striding along through the town square, on his way to lunch at the Campus Cafe. He nodded to Caddy the cop, who had parked his motorcycle at the curb and was idly surveying the square, squinting against the bright November sunshine. Caddy touched the brim of his helmet and the judge was walking on when someone shouted his name.

Judge Holmsby turned. A blue convertible was crossing the square. Merlin was at the wheel and Jen sat beside him, bright and pretty as a new penny. "Hi, Judge Holmsby," called Merlin. Jen waved.

The judge grinned and waved back, and Merlin stepped on the gas. A bright green cloud billowed out from the back of the convertible.

"Are you gonna let him get away with that?"

Caddy and the judge looked around. Norman Powell had stepped out of the Midvale Men's Shop just in time to see the convertible round the corner, trailing its green vapors behind it.

Judge Holmsby gave Norman a steely stare and the football player reddened and moved away. But he put his question again to Caddy. "I said, are you gonna let him get away with that?" he demanded. "Green exhaust! You saw it. That's creating a traffic hazard. Aren't you gonna give him a ticket?"

Caddy shook his head. "I don't think so," he said. "There's nothing in the vehicle code that says exhaust's got to be gray. Besides, I think colored exhaust looks kind of nice."

With that, Caddy gunned his motorcycle and roared away, leaving a cloud of purple smoke in his wake.

"I think," said Judge Holmsby, "that I prefer the green myself." And he walked on to get his lunch.

Whitman
CLASSICS

Whitman ADVENTURE and MYSTERY Books